ANATHEMA

Just Deserts Book One
By
Gwen Day

ANATHEMA PAPERBACK

First edition. November 5, 2022.

ISBN: 978-1739156046

Written by Gwen Day.

Dedication

To the readers who can see through the red flags and the morally grey to what is beneath, and understand why it fascinates us, in fiction.

Note

The Greek root of *anathema* originally meant simply "a thing de-voted" or "an offering," and in the Old Testament it could refer to either revered objects or objects representing destruction brought about in the name of the Lord, such as the weapons of an enemy. Since the enemy's objects therefore became symbols of what was reviled or unholy, the neutral meaning of "a thing devoted" became "a thing devoted to evil" or "curse."

In the early Church, *anathema* was used interchangeably with *excommunication* and to refer to unrepentant heretics. It then came to mean the severest form of excommunication in official church writings. When the authority of Rome was split in the Great Schism between Eastern and Western churches in 1054, an anathema was issued by Rome against the Eastern Patriarch who then issued another one against the cardinal who delivered it.

Merriam-Webster Dictionary

Despite its pronunciation, *just deserts*, with one *s*, is the proper spelling for the phrase meaning "the punishment that one deserves." The phrase is even older than *dessert*, using an older noun version of *desert* meaning "deserved reward or punishment," which is spelled like the arid land, but pronounced like the sweet treat.

Merriam-Webster Dictionary

Trigger Warnings

This is a work for mature audiences only, it contains graphic scenes of murder, torture, execution and assault. There are rough sexual scenes and off page childhood trauma.

Read with care. Please. Reading is meant to be fun, not endurance.

Prologue - Six Months Ago

Pain screams inside me and I smile through it, blood on my teeth, rain on my face, icy and cold, night all around me, as is fitting.

Blue and white strobes in the periphery of my vision, splintered by the rain, accompanied by the cacophony of approaching sirens, but I don't take my eyes off my target - prey - quarry - victim.

He never takes his eyes off me either, and he moves faster than I would have expected, snaking through shadows and reflections, as at home in the darkness as I am.

He's caught me once already. Aimed for my eyes but missed. I ducked the swipe he planned to blind me with and his knee hit me in the face as he spun, hence the blood I spit onto the cobbles.

Headlights wash the walls of the narrow alleyway and I see him clearly, bent over, a tall man getting low, altering his centre of gravity, masking his deadly reach.

You don't fool me, I've seen you kill, it was dramatic and accomplished, it's why I am giving you a chance.

Voices rise above the white noise of the rain, ordering us to freeze.

"Stand down, this is a Societal Justice issue." Despite her age and exhaustion Rose's voice crackles with authority. Her job is to deal with the audience, I deal with the animal in the ring.

I shake the blood and the water from my eyes and the voice of the pain settles into an enchanting chorus, stroking my nerves and muscles to performance peak.

He comes out of the edges of the night, low and quick like the rabid dog they named him for. The Mad Dog killer, all teeth and claws, trying to rend one last victim.

The sharp hooks attached to his gloved hands slice through my flesh before I can dance out of the way, playing piano on my ribs, the cuts so clean I don't feel them, and I mourn that.

He wants to kill me with a thousand cuts. I want to rip his throat out with my teeth.

Maybe he still thinks he can get away.

They all tend to think that. Those that have a god complex, that think they are the top of the food chain, right up until the end they think they will escape.

I encourage that way of thinking.

It adds to the fun.

"Too slow, instrument." His voice is for me alone. "I'm going to take you apart, and then I'll go after your steward, cut the old woman into dog meat."

His words make no impression. They are just noise, like the rain and the distant shouts, and the whomp whomp of rotor blades overhead.

A ghetto bird swings its lamp into the alley and the Mad Dog crouches lower, so used to hiding.

I move like the rain, inevitable. My hand in his hair spins him into the spotlight he always wanted, my height and weight pull him off balance, my foot in the back of his legs causes him to collapse to his knees. I follow it with a double elbow strike, hitting each side of his neck - his clavicles snap like chicken bones and his deadly hands hang useless.

The spotlight on us is white, like a tunnel to heaven.

I settle behind him, reaching around his skinny body, taking a firm grip on his wrists. He screams when his own hooks on his own hands disembowel himself and his guts squirm out into the night, fleeing the scene as it were.

I give him a moment to appreciate the justice, and then I snap his neck.

Adrenalin pumps through me, pain swings into a glorious chorus, hallelujah all the way, and slowly I rise to my feet. I look up into the light of the chopper and it flinches away from me, leaving me in the soothing sodden darkness.

I move down the alley to where Rose stands with the cops.

"You fucking call that justice?" The cop who speaks to her is green and pasty white, maybe it's the light, maybe it's what he just saw.

"No, we call it revenge, we don't play with words," Rose says coldly.

He looks at me like I am some sort of anathema, like I'm an unholy thing that crawled out of hell into the pure light of his kind of justice. He's not far wrong, and I don't care.

It's good for someone to see me, the real me, for once. I spend my life wearing masks among the normals, and it's tedious, it's good to let the real me out, for once. It's good to see the look on their faces, the fear in their eyes. The fear isn't because of my title, it's because of what I am.

I trigger people, when I let them see the real me.

Something down deep in their DNA sparks - run and hide.

Their blood recognises what I am - predator, alpha, psycho.

The cop takes a step back and I sneer at him, give him the benefit of my amber eyes and my bloody teeth.

He hisses, like part of him wants to ward me off, make the sign of the cross, twist his fingers to banish the evil eye, but the modern man can't quite remember how.

"Stop playing!" Rose snaps. She glares at me through the falling rain, five foot four of ageing rage and iron will. The closest thing I have to family. "We're leaving, they can clean this up."

I don't feel any regret for the meat gradually cooling under the cloudburst and the overflow of gutters, it's inside getting washed by the rain, even though he nearly got me.

He only got this close because I let him. It made it interesting. I got to kill in the open and that amuses me, arouses me, intrigues me.

Rose calls it playing with my food.

The rain drums on the roof of the SUV, tinny and tympanic. Rose grunts when she climbs in.

"You botched the capture on purpose. That didn't need to happen out in the open."

I say nothing, watching the raindrops explode into diamond mist when they land. It is like the whole world is exploding, violent and beautiful.

"Don't fall victim to overconfidence. It would be a stupid way to end, after everything."

I still say nothing.

Rose's short grey hair is plastered to her skull by the rain, the little bits of makeup she deigns to wear disintegrated by the hours and the storm.

"I'm too old for this St John."

"Obviously."

"You have to accept someone new, I am too old to be your steward, and I have other work to do, equally important work."

"Find me someone who will endure then."

She stares out at the night, at the scurrying officers in their slickers and self-righteousness, the flashing lights starbursting off them. Finally she sighs and reaches for the ignition key. "Do you need a doctor?"

Pain runs a loving hand over my nerve endings, sending conflicting signals to my wrongly wired brain. The arousal that bedded in during the fight straightens up and fills me, hot in my belly, tight in my thighs.

My cock thickens in my pants, and my mouth waters for fresh meat.

"No, just get me something to fuck."

Chapter One

St John

I wake no less irritated than when I went to sleep. Frustration and arousal are rolling at a low-level simmer in my brain and my body. I should have sought a release, but I couldn't decide if I needed to hurt or be hurt.

Normally, I know exactly what I want.

Watching the kill turned me on; it always does. There was pain involved, and although I was fifteen feet away I could feel it, smell it, almost taste it as the wire of the garrotte carved through the dirty skin of the neck.

The laziness of the killer had confused my arousal. He was sloppy, a random victim, no finesse, no evolution in technique, no learning or adapting.

The pain on the victim's face had caused a jerk in my limbic system, my cock going half-hard, my blood sluggishly stirring, but the lacklustre carry through from the killer snuffed out the fire inside.

I know I will be a lot harder when I kill him.

The pleasure will last much longer.

The best I can say about last night's kill was that it was quick, a blessing for the victim.

It was the second time I'd seen this killer perform, and the previous operation had been no more inspiring than this one.

I roll out of bed. I have time for a shower before watching the congressional committee do their annual rehashing of old issues before failing to find a way out of the ethical corner they have backed themselves into.

It is essential viewing. It gives me insight into which way the wind is blowing on Capitol Hill concerning my employment and, more than that, my existence.

Chances are the wind will still be gusting in my direction. The public remains fascinated and frequently aroused by people like me. But they remain reluctant to face the unpalatable truth that the human genome throws us up for a reason, and that reason is survival.

Apart from that, it's always amusing to watch the Director deliver this year's version of her '*You can't handle the truth*' monologue.

Under the warm water of the shower, I again feel the urge to give in to the sexual side of my issues, but it's not worth it. It won't assuage the itch, and I still can't decide between pain for myself, or hurting someone else.

Sometimes, when the disconnect is bad, I look down at my body, and I am surprised because it isn't what I expect to see. I see smooth lean muscle and length when I expect skinny, short, and dirty, with old blood on the backs of my legs, grime ground into too pale skin, and ribs like a toast rack.

The curling arousal makes it worse. Cuts me loose in time, sending me back to what I once was - powerless. I need to kill, or this vision of me becomes the more prevalent one. That isn't helpful; it takes the confidence away.

I don't have bad memories per se; I just had my evolution forced, so the real me, the me now, sometimes regresses. If I look in the mirror, I see both of us, the grown instrument and the tortured child, one standing inside the other.

Once I get my new steward and deal with this killer, it will be so much clearer, and I'll take my release with clarity and passion.

Rubbing my hair dry, I walk naked into the bedroom and flick on the TV. The committee is coming to order, the Director adjusting her microphone smoothly on the desk in front of her. I honestly don't know how she has the patience for this, but then we have different mentalities. Her various assistants congregate behind her, all dark shiny graduates of the Stewardship program. They look like a row of very expensive funeral directors, which is essentially what they are.

I pay little attention to the Stewards normally. Sometimes I can't tell them apart, they all have that blank corporate look. I certainly don't know their names or their histories.

Over the last few years Rose has sent me new ones, in an effort to engineer a replacement. I find them lacking, they leave. Sometimes they leave bleeding, sometimes they just leave crying.

I understand that we are supposed to bond with them, become a team with them, but who the hell thought that was a good idea? We are killers, we don't play well with others, that's kind of the point of us.

Rose has insisted this time will be different. We will see. I might try a little harder to find one that I can tolerate now Rose has insisted she can't do fieldwork anymore.

If the worst comes to the worst I suppose I could mould one to my specification - like Rose but more compliant, complicit, controllable, and quiet.

Quiet is essential. I loathe noise, no matter what I am working on.

Then we can get the show back on the road, and I can finally let the curling, aching need inside find its path to completion.

Natalie

We do this every year, and I have to admit I like it. My boss is a badass. But then, she would be, my boss is psycho-in-chief to a cabal of killers.

This will likely be my last time here for a year or so. There is no way I can avoid fieldwork for much longer, even with India as an excuse. My little sister is creeping into puberty now; she's all theirs now until the final decision is made. I no longer need to be close to the offices to provide familial support.

They want me in the field, and I'm not looking forward to it. I would rather stay on this side of the line, but there is no choice. I'm on a fast-track program to the top, and to get there, I need to actually work with an instrument, or get out.

I glance around the blue-painted room with the excessively patterned carpet and the hideous yellow swags at the tall windows. It's a good turnout, as usual. The fascination with our work remains high among the public. There are a couple of eager new faces on the ten-man committee who will be hoping to make their mark by sparring with my boss.

"Welcome to this in-camera session of the United States Government Oversight Committee on Ethics and Punishment, Congresswoman Albany Thorne in the chair."

The buzz in the room quietens, and I mentally square my shoulders.

Congresswoman Thorne knows the score here, but she likes to watch the less experienced be politely savaged. Sweetly smiling, the red-haired Senator from Washington State bangs her gavel and settles back in her chair.

"Now is the time to ask your annual round of questions of the Head of the Societal Justice Program, Dr. Mary Goodlove," she tells her fellow committee members. "Please try to be less inane than in previous years."

God love her, she's warned them, but they never listen.

From my seat directly behind my boss, I can see no tension in her pose, just the usual resolute confidence. She sits quietly, alone at the large desk, and ignores the clicking of the photographers on their knees around her table trying to get an interesting shot of her fascinating face.

I, and the rest of her assistants, emulate her, a row of calm, serious, smart subalterns primed to do a difficult job.

Serial killers are rarely stupid. Even the most arrogant know that the chances of being caught are high, particularly the more they kill. Eventually, they get their day in court. The final curtain call, the grand finale, for many of them it's a delicious idea. It's an opportunity to bask in front of the cameras, drink in the pure, cool pleasure of the agony of relatives, to relive the glory days. All with the slim, tantalising chance of an OJ moment, and they'd get away with everything.

We stopped all that. The Department I work for makes sure that doesn't happen. Every human interaction is an exercise in power, and we took their power away.

Our department is now judge, jury, and executioner, to the very, very few who qualify. Capital punishment is our remit. We administer the death sentence, and only the death sentence. We don't accept appeals, we don't drag out the process and nobody gets clemency once found guilty.

We also do it quietly. The intention is that the only time we are seen in public is during hearings like this. That doesn't always work, but it mainly works.

Every year we come here, and my boss answers the oversight committee's questions to justify how we administer the ultimate punishment.

Only two people are involved in the process. An instrument to investigate and carry out the sentence, and a steward to oversee the process.

The committee's first questions are the usual innocuous recaps of numbers and kills - how many Instruments, how many Stewards, how many victims received justice.

Then the more interesting stuff is raised.

The chair recognizes a first-term Congresswoman. She obviously didn't read the briefing pack properly as she says, "But what about justice being seen to be done? Justice has to be known in order to be effective. How are the victims to feel a sense of closure if everything takes place in secret?"

Dr Goodlove's face doesn't flicker, her dark eyes behind her round small glasses don't betray any emotion, her tone is even and calm as she leans forward to speak into the desk microphone. "It is. We send the families a letter – it says the killer of their son or daughter, wife or mother, husband or lover, has been dealt with by the Societal Justice Program. Everybody knows what that means."

"But what about closure?" She persists in deploying the cliché.

"There is no such thing as closure. There is only moving forward."

"But don't the families want details? Don't they want to know the circumstances of how their loved one died? Why they died? Was the killer remorseful? Don't they want the whole truth so they can process it?"

We go over the same ground every year, but as Dr Goodlove maintains to us, it's worth repeating. Everybody needs to understand why this is done and how it is done. Hopefully this is the only insight they ever get.

"Of course the families have questions and they are entitled to them, but if our services were called upon in pursuit of the killer, they know the circumstances of their relative's death were likely to be unfortunate."

"But you let them have the details?"

"Eventually. We pay for therapy, prepare them, and when at least two years have passed since the matter was in the care of an instrument, we will, under carefully controlled and supportive conditions, go through the circumstances with them if they wish. We are very fair."

"And the method of execution?"

"It is various," Dr Goodlove says firmly.

"How do you know what happens? How do you know that your tame psychopaths are not just doing their own thing? Whatever they fancy doing."

Goodlove allows herself a smile. "I take issue with the word *tame*. Our psychopaths are not tame. And everything they do is overseen."

"That must be a helluva job! It makes me wonder how you manage to get people to do it," says the elderly Congressman from New Jersey, trying and failing to lighten the mood.

"That would be one of the reasons why we were created, so that the right people with the right training oversee these matters, but you would be surprised how many applicants we get. We accept only one in a thousand to the Stewardship program. It is actually harder to get Stewards than Instruments, and the attrition rate is very high."

"Turns out they don't have the stomach for it?"

"Either that, or they like it too much." Dr Goodlove makes an elegant gesture of dismissal, which shows what she thinks of those who get to like their job too much.

I can't see it happening to me, I'm dreading the time I have to watch someone die.

"But the Stewards aren't psychopaths themselves?"

"That would defeat the object."

"Are you a psychopath, Dr Goodlove?" That's the congresswoman from Texas; she's been around the hill for what feels like forever. That must give her confidence because nobody has ever asked Mary Goodlove that straight out before.

Goodlove pauses before she answers. "In the strictest possible sense, yes, I am, as are many successful people. However, in the serial killer sense, no, I'm not, because I have no desire to do anything other than verbally spar with you. That is not illegal, currently"

The representative looks shocked. "But what if you suddenly got the urge? Have we placed a wolf to guard the henhouse?"

"The expression is a fox to guard the henhouse, madam, but even so, I am not very wolf-like. I care little for the pack other than in the most abstract sense. Besides, if I was going to evolve the desire to plait your entrails while you watched, I would have done so long ago given our interactions over the years."

There is a shocked laugh from the audience, and the Chair smothers a smile.

The polished and Hollywood bland gentleman from Delaware leans forward, his face all professional empathy. Slightly exaggerated, I feel. This isn't the stage or a movie; you don't need to overact. It's better if you don't; you look false on playback. Maybe it's the excitement of the topic that makes him forget to rein it in.

"Dr Goodlove," he says. Fair play to him, he has the debate voice nailed, a little bit of accent for colour, deep enough to make women other than me, touch their faces and fiddle with their hair. "As a former prosecutor myself, I have to stand up for the judicial system; for the rights of a person to be heard and judged by a jury. For due process. For the option of clemency. We're a civilized nation; we shouldn't be sanctioning justice at the hand of monsters. It's inhumane. Surely you agree there must be a better way?"

I know Dr Goodlove is smiling because I can see the Congressman's frown. That wasn't the response he expected.

"You find my question funny, Doctor?" His accent peeks through a little more.

None of us sitting behind our boss find the question funny. Despite knowing the answer, we all ask the question all the time.

"No, sir. I find your question fascinating, not least because it has already been asked in one form or another at every one of these meetings since this department was founded.

"To answer your question, yes, the judicial system would be a better way in theory, but we tried it and found that we can't trust you with it. You let colour, creed, background, and personal bias inform every decision you make. You operate within a system that is a game where the best lawyer wins. That is unacceptable in many ways; it is particularly unacceptable within the sphere of capital punishment.

"The people want the death penalty to be an option, that has been repeatedly made clear. Society cites anecdotal evidence that it is a deterrence. Society insists it should be allowed for amorphous reasons like justice. And the people demand it for frankly ridiculous reasons like revenge. It seems very many people want this but you cannot be trusted to administer it.

"Your system killed innocent people. It left the damaged and confused to linger in limbo in cement block prisons for decades while the game of clemency politics was played. It gave power to people who made their judgement based on vote numbers. It then passed the onus of carrying out your decisions on people who were ill-prepared to handle it. Your management of the system failed, so it was taken away from you.

"Now, only my department can apply the death penalty. We do so swiftly within a system that does not rely on opinion, public or otherwise.

"This system works because my Instruments have no bias, my Stewards are trained and supported, and our bar on proof is so high it makes reasonable doubt look like a crack in the sidewalk."

I am as transfixed by my boss as everyone else in the room. Her voice is even, and her words are clear. The certainty behind them, the barely reined in loathing of the confrontational system of the mainstream judiciary, is in every syllable.

"Change your judicial system, sir, take the death penalty off the books forever, and I, my Instruments, and my Stewards will gladly step down. But until you are willing to be human enough to do that we monsters will do the job we were born to do because we're better at it than you are."

Monsters, I walk with monsters. That's not an insult where I work; that's pretty much a job requirement.

My phone vibrates in my pocket, trembling against my breast. I slip it out of my jacket pocket and glance at it. The office knows I am here at the committee; it must be important if they are after me. Quietly, I slide from my place and slip away to return the call.

I could see this coming a mile off, but I hoped to have a few more months reprieve. It's not like I haven't trained for this, but there is an enormous chasm between training and reality. That's where the Stewards tend to bug out or burn out. Now I get to find out if I'm going to be one of those.

I've had a good run, a nice office job working directly with Dr Goodlove. I got to wear smart pants suits and never risk my skin. So far I've had an easy ride. The dirtiest thing I have had to do is keep up my fitness and take the occasional refresher in physical combat. I've never had to put on combats and get down in the dirt with the guilty, but that has to end if I want to make it to the top and have a hand in policy. I want that more than anything.

If Rose wants to see me, that can only mean one thing, I've finally been assigned an instrument.

It takes me an hour to get across town to our unobtrusive office building. The innocuous building with the heavy security sits beside a small park fenced with wrought iron railings, its trees wearing bright fall colours that are surprisingly cheerful.

I breeze through security and turn left to take the stairs to the administration offices. On the other side of the black and white checkerboard foyer there is additional security, manned by narrow eyed suits. They guard the entrance to the underground suites that house our arsenal, and the baby psycho school.

In the levels below our public offices young men and women determined to be potential Instruments are going through the process of determining where their terrible talents truly lie. It's where my own little sister is no doubt plotting ways to make my life difficult. It's her favourite hobby.

Rose's office is on the fourth floor, one level below the big boss who is currently driving the almost normals on the hill wild with frustration.

Rose has recently taken up the role of assigning Stewards after finally retiring from fieldwork. When I knock and let myself into her office it is still bare of personal touches, or perhaps she prefers a strict separation been home and work.

I've met Rose a number of times but it's hard to forget her fearsome reputation. Despite being a small, elderly woman I never get over just how focussed she is. She is all sharp corners and gimlet eyes, thin iron-grey hair combed back, a too-big nose, and her only adornment is the deep purple lipstick on her surprisingly wide mouth. Friendly is the last word you would use to describe Rose, but there isn't an empty seat in the room when she lectures at the steward program. She's been through the wringer, she's the real deal, and we're all in awe of her.

Rose nods at a seat in front of her desk and favours me with an assessing look. I suddenly realise which instrument I'm going to get.

Fuck my life. It's going to be St John Miller.

She can obviously read my body language like an open book because her face takes on a mocking cast. "You'd better up your game, pretty lady, because he's going to eat you for breakfast if you don't learn to bring your A-game."

I shake my head ruefully. "It's Miller, isn't it?" I press my lips together. "Who did I annoy enough to deserve that?"

She laughs, a rusty sound. "Yep, you get to replace me. Surely that makes you proud?"

What it makes me is close to wetting myself because St John Miller is legendary. A bare six months ago he took out a serial killer in plain sight, disembowelling the Mad Dog killer in front of half the DC police force before vanishing into the storm like Batman's nastier alter-ego.

I have spent a significant amount of time over the last six months working out how Dr Goodlove will handle that incident at the congressional oversight meeting. The only good thing about that fuck up was that nobody filmed him. Word of mouth is bad enough though.

Not only is St John the most efficient instrument the program has, but he's the original child prodigy and notoriously difficult to work with.

It was out of St John's deviant mind that the Early Onset program was born. He's the founding member of a very select and twisted club that now counts my little sister as a junior member.

"I suppose there isn't a chance that the assignment can be changed?" I try my well-honed charm on Rose but I haven't got a hope.

"Oh no, sweetcheeks, this comes straight from the top. You go to St John. Only the finest of fresh blood for my boy."

"Can we drop the derogatory monikers? I appreciate your seniority, but they aren't helpful."

"Fuck you, and what you think is helpful." Her black eyes look into my soul and clearly find me wanting. "You better learn to take that kind of shit because St John will throw far worse at you. St John will torment you just because he's bored, his coffee is cold, or he can't find the exact right word to translate into English from ancient Etruscan. Get used to it."

"You clearly think I am the wrong person for the job, so why don't you do us both a favour and throw your weight behind another steward? You were his permanent steward for years; surely they will listen to you?"

The rusty laugh rolls out again. "You are my choice, Natalie. You have always been my choice."

What the fuck?

"Now I am even more confused."

"I've been watching you for years. You have manipulated and charmed your way out of field work since you waltzed out of training top of your class. Even our glorious founder likes you and she likes less people than I do. But you signed up to be a steward, and I need someone with better than even odds of surviving St John. That's you."

"Should I feel flattered?" I couldn't help the bitter tone that crept into my voice.

"I don't give a shit what you feel." She slid a file across the desk to me. "All I care about is that the instrument I supported and trained from the very beginning gets a steward he can work with, and I sincerely hope that is you. Because if St John loses it completely with a steward and I have to retire him, I'm going to be very upset."

"If St John loses it with me I'll likely be dead, you being upset will be the least of my worries at that point," I point out.

"Yes, it would be too late for you, Natalie, but there is one other person who could suffer if you fail. That would be a shame, as she is doing well in the program."

"That was low," I say evenly, but my stomach tightens. It looks like Rose has no problem holding my sister's future over my head as a threat, and like all the baby psychos her future is precarious.

"I do what is necessary," Rose says bluntly, and I see the experienced steward in her eyes. Here is someone who has seen bloody death more than once and watched it all with her eyes wide open. I hope I never get that cold, but it seems unlikely.

"What if we just don't click?" I ask.

"Of that I have few doubts; you'll click alright."

"How do you know?"

"Because he will be both irritated, and fascinated by you. He worked with me because we had mileage. He will work with you because he'll want to work you out. Hopefully, he won't kill you to see exactly how you tick."

Goosebumps crawl up my arms at the way she says that, but I'm not going to give her the satisfaction of seeing my fear.

"When do I meet him?" I ask, as neutrally as possible.

"In about fifteen minutes. Read this file." She nods at the folder she slid across to me. "He has the results and the evidence on this case but we cannot proceed until he has his new steward. He will meet you, briefly, here in the office and then we'll take it from there. He is as unhappy with this as you are, but he has only seen you on paper. He will change his mind when he meets you in person."

Not if I can help it. This could be my only out.

She stands up, and I look questioningly at her. "Where are you going?"

"You meet him on your own, sweetheart. He does his own introductions. Just make sure you read that file thoroughly and quickly. He hates when people aren't prepared."

I glare at her.

She laughs again as she limps towards the door. She clearly thinks this whole situation is fucking hilarious. "You might thank me for this one day, Natalie, if you survive."

I roll my eyes and open the file. I have less than fifteen minutes to absorb this case file because I know St John will be on time; he's known for it – utterly efficient, totally ruthless, hyper intelligent, and twisted as a corkscrew.

I bend my head over the case notes and crime scene photos and within seconds I'm absorbed by the story. Never mind the reason I initially put myself on this path underneath it all is a fascination with the cases, with the people who die, and the people who kill them.

They are awful but they intrigue me, more than I ever thought they would.

For five whole seconds after he comes in through the door he fools me. He looks like a librarian. His hair is dark brown, neatly combed but thick, curling around his ears. He's of middling height and his wide eyes are hidden behind innocuous black-framed glasses. He's careful not to make eye contact.

His body language whispers, *nothing to see here, look away, everything is fine.*

And I fall for it. Just for those five seconds, I think this man has come to the wrong place. He's lost. He should be somewhere on level two where the records are, or maybe he has a meeting on level one with the HR people.

I'm just about to open my mouth and tell him he is in the wrong office when my training kicks in.

And then I see him. I see through him, through the subtle stoop to hide his height, the unfashionable hair and the nerd glasses, the purposely ill fitting clothes.

"That would have been long enough to kill you." His voice is low. There is grit and frustration there, grinding its gears.

What can I say? He's right. I was expecting him, and I still didn't see him.

Now it's obvious, and I can't believe I missed it.

Muscle groups move. He straightens, and he towers over me. His head comes up and the line of his jaw is sharp and square, arrogantly tilted. He looks down on me with disdain.

My eyes meet his and I see they are a strange, cat-like yellow and all I can think of is he's like a tiger, the tiger that burns bright in the forests of the night.

Under the cunning drabness of his suit, I can now see the lines of his grace. He is wide-shouldered and cat-lithe with the long smooth lines of a runner.

His hands are huge. The fingers long. The bones of his wrists could take a hammer blow.

He lets me look. He lets the whole facade slip so I can really see him.

He is, I find myself thinking, magnificent.

A moment ago, I thought him innocuous; now I see the predator. Not only that, I see the man, and he is hot as hell. His lips are full and his features symmetrical. But it is the way he moves that burns him into my brain and makes me realise I am in even more trouble than I thought.

Carefully telegraphing my movements, I rise from the chair and hold a hand out to him. A peace offering. A handshake. An attempt to bring him down to my human level.

He looks at my hand with complete disinterest.

"I don't see the point of that," he says. "It's a gesture of peace; I'm not peaceful."

A very fair point.

"We're not getting off to a good start, are we?" I say.

"No." He looks me up and down, and it's uncomfortable to be under that eerie gaze. "Did you read the file?"

"Yes, yes, I did," I nod vigorously. He is hard to make eye contact with, but I try and I give him my best focussed and enthusiastic gaze.

"And?"

"And what?"

"Recap," he says lazily.

He ignores me while I stutter through a brief summary of the case. He turns his back on me, fiddles with the files on Rose's desk, displaying blatant arrogance. Knowing what he is doing doesn't make it any less effective. He has me at such a disadvantage.

The case is not complicated, but that in itself is a problem. It appears the police had very little to go on - Six dead homeless people, three men, three women, found in various city parks over the last two months, all strangled with a wire, no sign of sexual assault, no apparent motive.

There had been no attempts to hide the bodies; they were left where they fell.

The case got passed to us because the methodology showed evidence of a single killer. The victimology, and the fact that the bodies weren't moved after death or interfered with in any way, meant forensics had zip to go on. I point this out in my summing up of the file.

St John takes a seat and looks at me. "You think the file got passed to us because it was expedient?"

I nod.

"You are probably right," he says, sounding bored. "But it is solved anyway; I have identified the killer."

I warily take my seat as well. "That was quick. They only sent it over two weeks ago."

"I solved it eight days ago; I've been waiting for you."

"Oh."

"Oh, indeed."

His yellow eyes peruse me at his leisure, gliding up and down my body, taking in my business attire, my bland white blouse, my less than sexy shoes – mid heel, easy to walk in. I feel like I'm being scanned.

"Tell me something about yourself, Natalie, something that wasn't in your file."

"My little sister is in the program," I confess the most personal thing about me, the strongest connection I have to him, the thing that has defined my last decade. The thing I usually keep very quiet.

He looks bored. "I don't care."

"Sorry, I thought you would be interested."

"Not in the slightest. Try again, something other than the obvious."

"Stop it, St John," Rose speaks from the doorway. "The purpose of this meeting wasn't for you to bait your new steward."

"I might not accept her."

"Yes, you will." She sounds weary. "We both know you will."

She steps into the room. St John rises and moves towards her. I tense, but he offers her an arm as she limps towards her desk.

"Leave it." She slaps his arm. "It's fine; it's just winter coming on. I'm not crippled."

St John returns to his seat, and Rose sits down with a sigh. "I would like to progress this case as quickly as possible. St John, are you willing to let Natalie come to your house to go over the evidence?"

"Yes." His voice is gentler with Rose; it lacks the snarky supercilious edge he used with me.

"And if that meeting goes well, will you accept her as your steward?"

St John drags it out, his eyes narrowed, his gaze on the floor. I find myself holding my breath. For some reason, I want him to say yes, and yet half an hour ago, I would have done anything to wriggle out of this.

"I will," he replies eventually.

"I would take it as a personal favour if you would play nice with her, St John," Rose says. There must be a personal message in her words because he flashes her a smile. He looks younger, more playful, less the tiger, more the cub.

"I can try," he says innocently.

There is a glaringly obvious bond between these two. Maybe it is a natural result of working a difficult job in partnership. If it is, will I have in-jokes with St John one day?

"Trying is good; doing is better," says Rose primly.

I sit there like a dumb idiot, waiting to be included.

It is St John who turns to me. His face is more relaxed and his expression less intimidating. "I have the evidence ready. Shall we say 8 a.m. at my house tomorrow morning? We can discuss it and take it from there."

"Of course, Sir, I'll be there." I feel the need to have him recognize me, notice me as someone about to be a significant presence in his life. "I hope we find a way of working together, I've heard so much about your work."

"Everyone here has heard about my work," he says.

"Yes, and I was up until 4am trying to come up with a less vomit worthy way of describing your work with the Mad Dog Killer." My mouth betrays me, despite all my efforts to make myself into Miss Diplomatic it tends to do that. I like to think it's the added salt for flavour in my personality.

"She's mouthy. Is she a brat?" St John asks Rose.

"No, just lacking in mileage, I'm sure you will correct that deficiency."

"Undoubtedly." He looks me over again and there is a spark of interest in his tourmaline eyes. "You can call me Sin," he says.

It suits him. He is sinfully attractive, but more than that he is every tempting bad thing. I don't know if I am adult enough to resist sin like him.

He gives a mocking smile and stands, pulling his coat around himself. It is almost like he vanishes. The tiger fades away into the undergrowth, and there is just an ordinary man standing there with a cute tilt to his head and a shy demeanour.

He nods at Rose, and leaves quietly. I let out a breath I didn't know I was holding. "He is something else," I say.

"Yes," agrees Rose. "And we're still trying to work out exactly what something else he is. He must like you though, you're not on the way to the emergency room and he gave you his preferred name. Most don't get that far."

That doesn't fill me with a whole heap of confidence.

"Why does he pronounce his name that way?" I ask. I think I am desperate to prolong this conversation, to get more insight on my new instrument.

"It's a family tradition. It has been pronounced sin-jun for multiple generations as I understand."

There is a brief knock on the door and Baldwin enters. His appearance gives me confidence. He was my close combat instructor when I was in training and being high up in support services he generally oversees my routine refreshers. He's a massive black man with a dry sense of humour once you get past his tendency to double dot his eyes and right angle cross his tees.

He's always seemed to approve of me, and it boosts me to see him.

"Take a seat," Rose says, "As you know Natalie has been assigned to St John. I thought your insight into working with him might be useful."

I glance at Baldwin, he has a scar that runs down his face. It's thick and gnarled and makes his expression grim, tugging his mouth down at the side. He also has a depression in his bald skull.

Rumour has always been rife amongst the Stewards as to how he got his scars.

Baldwin gives me a sympathetic look. "I'm happy to help," he says, "Seeing as St John was how I got these little reminders for life."

"You worked with him?"

"I lasted a single morning."

"Why did he do this to you?"

"He doesn't play well with others," Rose said, "But specifically he doesn't like men much."

"Is that why I was drafted in, because he prefers women?"

"It isn't that he prefers them, he just seems less inclined to damage them so badly."

"Clearly a gentleman."

"No," Baldwin's voice is a low grumble, "He isn't a gentleman, he just doesn't feel the need the impress them in quite the same way."

"Whores or Madonna complex?" I query.

"We have no idea. We have no idea what labels to attach to him, he doesn't really fit any of them." Rose says. "He never did."

I guess once you swim into this end of the gene pool the water is deep and murky, nobody fits neatly into boxes, I know my sister doesn't and she is about as classic a psychopath as you can get.

They are all down there swimming and killing each other, just below the surface of the mass of humanity, the outliers and the mutated, the born and the made, snapping their jaws and tearing each other apart, while the rest of us navigate the sunny topside, mainly oblivious.

"I'll take any advice I can get?" I say.

"My best advice is never turn your back, never assume he's fine and take advantage of all the supervision Rose offers," Baldwin says.

I was hoping for something more concrete.

Chapter Two

St John

When my alarm sounds, I reluctantly lay down my pen and bring myself back to the modern world with a moment of mindfulness. I'm not some hippy-dippy, inward-looking, navel-gazer, but I find it helps me move from one aspect of my life to another, particularly when I am working in ancient Greek and need to go back to thinking in English.

I feel the smooth wood of the desk beneath my fingers.

I see the frame of the window painted green.

I hear the rumbling thrum of the drier in the laundry room next door.

It would not be wise to make a habit of this kind of centering, but it's a little indulgence I allow myself when I am working on things related to my day job. In my other work, I would never permit it; that way lies death.

I feel the warm air from the vents blowing across my bare feet.

I see the golden goat from Akrotiri.

I hear the fan on my computer whir to life.

Calm, my mind is calm. I breathe out long and slow and get up and stretch.

Natalie will be here soon.

I wonder how I will react to having another person into this space where so few come.

Change, Rose tells me it is good for me, and that it will not negatively impact any of my work, but change is a difficult thing. Rose has been with me for so long, and Natalie is a radical change.

She didn't look like her paper profile suggested. I imagined someone smaller, more bookish, softer around the edges. I could have looked up more about her before we met, but I couldn't be bothered at the time, I was too irritated.

She was taller than I thought she would be, stronger looking, with the curves of a woman not a girl. With the training she has received she should be an ally, a potential back-up in my kill room, and that makes me feel tense in a way I need to examine - I don't think I want to share my work, even if necessary. Like Rose says, I do like to play with my food, but that doesn't mean I want it taken from me.

Rose's limp is a left over from playing with my dinner. I suppose I should regret that. I try, just to see if I can, but I can't. She should have stood further back. She didn't lose the leg. She can walk. Not my problem. The man died screaming. I feel a shimmer of arousal at the memory.

Natalie entered the steward training program straight out of college, so she has no experience in the real world. I suspect that there will be an innocence about her that will need to be eradicated. She's not like me, I had my innocence ground to dust before I even hit puberty.

I flick through the case file on my desk. Her first stewarding will knock a few of the rounded curves off her personality, temper her a bit.

Again there is a dark curl of arousal in my stomach when I think of the case I am about to bring to a conclusion. It always comes when the time draws near. I have been tamping it down while waiting for my new steward to be assigned, but now the animal inside me is swishing his tail, crouched and waiting, hissing through his teeth at the play to come.

In this instance, I don't think it is just the execution that arouses me; that will be routine. The case is tedious, it took me very little work to find the perpetrator, and the man is an idiot. But his execution will be enhanced by Natalie's presence. Physical pain may be the main arousal trigger but mental pain, that's tasty too, and my new steward is going to hurt during this, it's inevitable with the normals.

All the evidence is in order, I very much doubt there will be any holdup in rubber-stamping the kill, but Natalie will have to run this by Rose as it is our first case together. Not that it's really a case, I've done all the heavy lifting. Natalie is just along for the inevitable conclusion.

I suppose I had better change my clothes before Natalie gets here. She won't be late, she's too scared of me to be tardy.

No doubt she will feel comfortable enough to risk it at some point, but not today. Arousal stirs. When the time comes, I can punish Natalie for her tardiness, impudence, and errors in ways I would never dream of with Rose.

Maybe change won't be so bad after all.

I strip off my sweat pants and t-shirt in the laundry room that forms part of my office annex. Along with my large office and the laundry, the annex has a guest bedroom and a full bath that Rose used when she stayed over. I suppose Natalie will use these rooms now, if she stays, if we can work together effectively.

Briefly, I wonder if Rose has given Natalie the "What St John likes to do afterward," talk yet.

That makes me smile; I don't think she will be expecting that.

It will be just one of the many things they don't cover in training.

Welcome to the world of the sanctioned killer, Natalie, where the only real payment we receive is intellectual and physical; there's no money in this game.

I go through the clean clothes stacked next to the dryer, ready to be taken upstairs to my rooms. Black jeans and a black long-sleeved Henley will do. I'm not wearing a disguise today; I'm just being me.

It never ceases to amaze me how the slim disguises I slip on actually work. Natalie was fooled by just my clothing and body language when I met her, and she was expecting me. She wasn't fooled for long, but long enough, if there had been a need for it.

It seems that people are either really short-sighted or lack the imagination to see the killers that lurk amongst them.

I am not hampered in that way. I have a good imagination, although it is a single-lane highway. It only has one destination - the truth of the kill. I can feel the motive and the payoff for those who kill. I can imagine the planning and the execution of the killer, and more usefully, I imagine the errors the killer will make, and they are usually correct.

With regard to my life, I have no imagination. It isn't required.

I have my day work, which is fascinating.

I have my other work, which is intriguing and satisfying.

I have lust, pain, greed, and orgasmic pleasure in exactly the way I want them.

What else would a high-functioning psychopath need?

Nothing. The answer is clearly nothing.

Having dressed, I pull on a pair of boots and run my hands through my hair. Natalie will be here in exactly three minutes, of that I am sure.

She may well be loitering outside the gate, but she won't arrive until the exact moment. Not early, not late. A generous man would assume Natalie will be on time because she wants to make a good impression, start our working relationship on an efficient foot. I'm not a generous man. Natalie will be on time because she is scared of me, and so far, apart from a little needling in a safe environment, she is scared of me purely based on my reputation.

I would prefer she was scared of me because of what I had done to her, that tastes nicer in my head. I consider making the coming meeting difficult for her, just to see how she reacts, but that would be counterproductive. This case has been held up long enough. It's time for justice to be done.

I am no avenging angel - never, ever, ever that. Nothing angelic about me; I have the proof. But I do specialise in killers that prey on the underclass, the dispossessed and unnoticed, because they deserve representation as much as a rich man's son. And this particular killer has preyed long enough on those who fall through the cracks in society. It is time to end him.

Making my way through the sunny, bright foyer of my house, I open the front door and lean against it just as Natalie arrives at the step.

Natalie

St John's house is nothing like I expected. For a start, it's the least sinister property I have ever seen, and it's in the nicest area of the city. Not flashy nice, but seriously quaint nice.

On a narrow one-way street, facing a park, St John's house sits in the centre of a row of townhouses that step down a gentle hill in an irregular run of differing heights, differing sidings, and differing materials. Some are painted wood, some pastel render. St John's house is warm red brick. The houses are all cute, well-kept. Their varying colours and pretty wooden trim make it an area brimming with character and charm.

My Mother would have adored it.

The entrance is through a dark green metal gate and along a narrow paved walkway bordered on either side by low-growing herbs and high walls. Brick steps lead up to a shiny green door. St John is already there, leaning on the door frame, wearing black jeans and a form-fitting Henley with four buttons at the neck. The shirt clings to his physique, highlights his shoulders, and the sleeves are pushed up to show well muscled forearms.

He doesn't speak, just steps aside. I enter a sunlit white foyer with a golden hardwood floor and mouldings painted a pale grey.

It is a beautiful and peaceful space. Through open double doors, I catch a glimpse of a living room bathed in light and white painted stairs leading to the upper floor. St John leads me to the right and into an annex that runs parallel to the entrance path. "This is my working area," he says. I follow him into a spacious office full of immaculately ordered books, manuscripts, and paper, all of varying degrees of age.

"Rose told me you're a translator when you aren't working on cases." All Instruments have a day job, both to give them a real presence in the normal world and because it's essential to keep them occupied as much as possible.

"Sort of; I decipher ancient manuscripts, tablets, and inscriptions. I specialise in Linear B, and I am part of a research team on Linear A, but I also work in other languages as time permits."

I must have looked confused - who wouldn't?

"Linear A and B are ancient languages from the Minoan civilization which flourished in what is now Crete over three and half thousand years ago."

"Oh." I'm clearly a master of small talk. "Sounds really interesting."

"Yes, I can tell you exactly how many jars of olive oil were given as tribute to a certain priestess three and a half eons ago," St John replies, deadpan.

I hunt for something to say. "Have you spent much time there? Crete, I mean."

He speaks slowly, as if to a child. "No, Natalie, I'm not allowed to leave the country, remember?"

Fuck, rookie mistake. I kick myself mentally. Instruments don't have the freedom the rest of us enjoy. The world, to a larger degree, is locked to them. They can pass as normal, but they can never be normal.

"Sorry," I say, and I mean it. Looking around his office, there are signs everywhere that he would love to travel, at least to the parts of

the world that had really old civilizations. There are framed sepia photographs of archaeological sites on one wall, models of wooden sailing
ships on a shelf above the sofa, and ancient-looking artefacts in cubby
holes.

St John picks up a little gold-colour goat that he has been using as
a paperweight; it looks tiny in his large hands. He strokes it delicately.
"Yeah, me too. It would have been nice to see the things I have spent
decades studying." And that's the first time he has shown any emotion
other than irritation.

"Where would you go if you could travel?" I quietly sit on the sofa.
I want to know him better. We're going to do intense things together,
and it would help if I found a way to connect with him other than fear.

For a moment, I think he isn't going to answer.

"Akrotiri. There is a dig there into an ancient city buried under vol-
canic ash. They think it might have been Atlantis. I'd go there first. I
want to see the wall frescoes."

He suddenly puts the little gold goat back. "Don't try to be my
friend, Natalie. It's pointless. But thank you for asking, it was polite of
you to show an interest in my other occupation."

I nod, but despite his words, maybe I've made a little headway.

"Would you like coffee first, or shall we get straight into it?"

"Are we on any sort of timescale?" I ask, and he shakes his head.
"Coffee first then." I grin. "I need to know how you like your coffee so
I can bring it with me sometimes."

"I never drink coffee shop coffee."

"You're going to be hard work, aren't you?" I try to tease him.

"Like you wouldn't believe," he says, and then gestures at the doorway. "Come on, I'll give you the tour. Then we can review the evidence,
and I can, hopefully, go kill someone."

I nearly laugh, but he's not kidding. That is what we are going to do
today.

Suddenly, I'm really fucking nervous again.

St John sits down behind his desk. He has a nice chair, big, black leather, heavily cushioned.

He sees me looking. "I spend a lot of time on my ass; I might as well be comfortable."

I choose the sofa again. "How do you normally do this?" I ask. They teach us that the Instruments have their routines, their ways of doing things, and we should try and fit in with that as much as possible. It keeps them relaxed, which is apparently the best way for your instrument to be.

An uptight instrument is a dangerous instrument, and the steward is the closest relationship most of them have. They have a tendency to take their stresses out on us; it's one of the many reasons Stewarding has a high attrition rate.

St John is looking at me quizzically.

"Did you and Rose have any set routine, a way of doing things that you would like to keep doing?" I explain because he doesn't seem to understand.

"Oh, you're trying to make me comfortable."

"I'm trying to minimise the amount of change for you. I know that change can be stressful."

"What's stressful is you behaving like a robot; be yourself."

"I'll give it a go."

"Your name comes from the latin phrase natale domini, it translates as birth of the lord and is name associated traditionally with fresh starts and rebirth."

I blink, "How do you know that?"

"Ancient languages," he shrugs, "In the same way that I know Chicago means skunk in Algonquin"

I laugh, I can't help myself, it bursts from me at the expression on his face, the way his nose wrinkles, it's kind of cute. His mouth smiles, but his eyes are cold, like a winter sun setting over frozen fields, and I realise he is playing me.

It worked, I realise I am more relaxed.

We stare at each other - I feel like I am taking the first steps in a dance I'm not familiar with and he has led me into it. I'm not sure how that makes me feel. Confused mainly, that he bothered, because that isn't the St John I was led to expect.

He leans back in the seat. "You remember the initial file?"

I nod.

"Here are the conclusions from my investigation." He pushes a folder across the desk towards me.

When I reach for it, he looks disappointed.

"What?" I ask, my hand hovering over the buff folder.

"I could just tell you?"

"You could, but I will still have to review the actual evidence."

"You won't like the evidence."

"Is it photographic?" I keep my voice even, but he's right, I'm dreading that part.

"Yes."

I push the folder away and lean back on the sofa. "Maybe I should work up to that. Tell me first."

St John tells me a story of a killer and his victims.

Maybe this is a routine he doesn't want to admit to liking. Maybe he likes to verbalise his investigation or he simply enjoys telling stories.

Perhaps he gets to speak to so few people that this is a subconscious desire on his part. Maybe I'm full of shit, and he just gets off on it. Whatever the reason, he is mesmerising.

He sits back in his chair, and his low voice reaches out, grabs me, and immerses me in his storytelling. It's almost as if the killer takes form before me, stepping out of the darkness into a spotlight of Sin's creation, emerging in 3D, holding his murder weapon of choice casually in his hand.

Cawston is our killer. Cawston is a frustrated man, a personal trainer who once had a wife with whom he wanted to play kinky games. She wasn't so keen, and got a bit upset when he wanted to choke her while he fucked her. He'd heard, in a locker room somewhere, where guys lie to each other, that it would make her pussy tighter.

She got a bit upset because she thought her pussy was plenty tight, and she got a bit upset because Cawston was a big guy, and she rightly figured that he wouldn't know when to stop.

She confided this to the sweet little Thai girl who does her nails, who listens, nods, and spits out curses about filthy men while she lacquers ladies' toes - she told me all this while she played with my feet for an hour, money well spent, I felt.

Cawston told his wary wife that he would learn to choke her safely, and off he went to practice.

Grounds for divorce thought wifey, and her lawyer thought the same. Divorce granted.

But in the meantime, Cawston practiced in case another wife came along. He is, from hacking his porn, fascinated by what happened to the body when it fought for air.

He tried to choke a call girl in an alley while he fucked her - she clawed his face and warned her friends.

"Watch out for the jogger in the beanie and the bright Nikes."

She told me this while I passed out hot coffees and condoms one cold and quiet night, playing the part of just another earnest volunteer, trying to help the street people.

Cawston goes jogging in the parks of a night. When the police occasionally stop him, he dutifully jogs on the spot to show he's into his fitness and brags of tight-tushed housewives who like him to train them in the outdoors where more people can see their tone. He is always looking for spots to take them.

The officers laugh and say, "Some guys get all the luck," and go back to pounding their beat and sweeping up the strangled vagrants. Cawston puffs out his puffed-up chest and carries on.

When I looked through the records properly, I found eighteen victims over two years, not the six the police attribute to this case. I also found two survivors.

Cawston took his first victim the day his divorce came through. An old woman, deaf, nearly blind, half-starved from life on the street; her neck must have snapped like a frozen twig. Minimal effort, minimal reward. Cawston did it again two weeks later - that one survived; I heard about it at a mobile soup kitchen where I handed out care packs.

I found the victim in the flophouse at the back of the Catholic Mission. He remembered a man trying to choke him. Took him from behind, he said, tried to use his bare hands - which is inefficient and difficult - but the old boy was tough; he'd been taken down too many times. He headbutted his assailant.

That night, Cawston attended the emergency room for a broken nose, and needed two teeth veneers fitted at his dentist.

The evidence is stacking up around Cawston, who is lazy, stupid, and barely worth my time. I find I dislike Cawston.

Cawston now has two markers on his scale for victim selection. The too easy and the too hard, but his choice of victim profile is perfect. Mainly by accident, I assume, or because the prostitute scared him. Anyway, vagrants become his prey of choice.

By this point he has long since stopped being fussy about the sex of his victims. The choking has stopped being about sex for Cawston; it's now all about power because he is powerless and diminished by his wife, and his job is menial according to the husbands of the wives he tones. He still jerks himself off to the idea of fucking and choking - I've seen him - but it's the killing that is the real payoff now. Its power over those he sees as lesser than himself.

The method he utilizes ties into one of the few things he is actually good at, he is physically strong and fit.

He chokes all of his victims in parks while out jogging. He graduated to the garrotte fairly recently; prior to that, he used variations on thin ropes. He is attached to the garrotte; he thinks it is exotic and gives him cool points, although it signalled him to our people because it became a signature in six kills.

Like I said, he is stupid.

When St John stops speaking, I let out a slow breath. Hearing him tell it is fascinating - I will reflect on it later. Right now, I have questions.

"All of this is in the file?"

"Yes."

"And the photographic evidence?"

"I have him on film killing two victims in the last couple of weeks."

"Two!"

"Once I had proof of him killing I marked the case as ready for execution and sent it for approval. In the time it took you to be assigned, he killed again."

"And you filmed that too."

"Yes, I continued to monitor him, but regretfully, the kill did not trigger the emergency protocol for intervention without approval."

In certain cases, instruments are allowed to step in and deal with a client without the evidence having been verified, but St John is right, this case does not meet that very narrow and specific criteria.

That criteria is overly harsh in my opinion. It would be something I would change if I made it to the top. The absolute proof of guilt demanded by the program is the worst thing about it as far as I am concerned.

I close my eyes briefly and push the sadness away - another human life snuffed out because of bureaucratic hoops.

"I can assure you it made me angrier than you," St John's voice is cold. "This is my case. These victims are mine to avenge; one more was not required to merit my punishment."

Each instrument has their particular type of case. St John's cases are assigned to him based upon victimology. He is invariably given the cases where the victims are the nameless and the lost, the people who fall through the cracks in society.

It is not that St John has a particular affinity for these people; it is exactly the opposite. We don't give instruments the kind of cases they would personally like to take because that would feed into their deviancy.

"Is all the evidence in the file?"

He nods and starts to fiddle with his computer. I feel his tolerance of me is wearing thin for the day. "The video files are on a drive attached to the file along with a pick-up strategy, timeline, and risk assessment for execution. If the case is green lit we can collect him tomorrow night."

I try to keep my face neutral.

In just over twenty-four hours, I could be watching a man die, painfully.

St John's eyes are on my face, and I watch him as he greedily assesses me. I feel like a bug under a microscope.

I brace myself mentally, expecting him to needle, to push, to lever at the edges of me, but he just turns away. The sunlight through the window catches his thick dark hair and highlights the lashes that are almost long enough to rest on his high cheekbones. He has the most beautiful profile.

"I'll take the file then, and I'll review it with Rose; she has to rubber-stamp my first case with you."

"Your first case, period."

"Quite, my first ever, cherry popping, never done this before, case."

He smirks. "Brave little steward."

I feel the hair on my forearms rise. He is the most unsettling man, but I think he almost likes it when I push back.

"I'll call you later, once I have spoken to Rose."

"Text me; I'll be busy."

I stand and take the file from his desk. He lounges back in his chair, then springs to his feet, and I flinch. Fuck, I need to get a grip.

"Stop it!" I snap at him. "We have to work together, stop playing with me."

He smiles, slow and easy. "You're starting to get interesting. Maybe Rose is right about you."

I have a feeling Rose has been right about a lot of things over the years. Hopefully, she won't mind sharing some insights if I play nice and figure out a way to charm her.

"You survived then." Rose looks up at me from her desk, her tone is acerbic, but her face tells a different story. She looks worn but stoic, her eyes shadowed.

She can't be looking forward to reviewing one more file from St John despite having gone through many with him. I guess you have to build whatever defences work to be around people like St John and situations like this, but I don't for one moment think it ever gets easy for her.

"Yes, he's got a nice place, not what I expected," I say. "Being a instrument must pay a lot more than being a steward!"

"No, it barely pays anything, and it's means-tested." She caps her pen and gives me her full attention. "Sin had a rich family."

"Had?"

"All gone now."

"Did he? Was he?" I stumble for words, not just because I don't know how to phrase it, but because of the way she looks at me. Like I am some sort of idiot.

"No and no. Now give me the fucking file so we can get this signed off."

My previous boss was a hard woman to work for and she was a straight-up high-functioning sociopath, but she was nothing compared to Rose. She makes me feel two inches tall, three years old, and like a puppy that has just shit on the floor, all at once. It's deeply unpleasant and momentarily makes me forget I am supposed to be trying to get in her good books.

I hand the file over and sit and wait while she flicks through it.

"Did he tell you a story?" she asks casually.

"Yes." St John's recounting of the evidence must be part of his ritual. She huffs.

"What's with that?"

"He likes stories; it's what makes him such a good investigator. Despite what he thinks, he's actually very good at connecting with people and getting information out of them." She reaches for the storage device and plugs it into her computer. "I don't think he even realizes how likeable he can make himself when he is ferreting out evidence.

"And he obviously doesn't loathe you, or he would have just given you the file. Telling you a story means he is interested in you and your reactions." There is a gentleness to her expression that I haven't seen before, a degree of softness when she talks about him.

She turns to her computer and sighs as she clicks the mouse. Thankfully, she keeps the sound turned down while the video evidence plays. I watched it before I gave it to her. The best thing I can say about it is that it is clear.

After a few minutes, she clicks the mouse again and takes off her old-fashioned square glasses, and rubs her eyes tiredly. "Did you watch this?"

I nod solemnly.

"Consider the execution rubber-stamped. I will message Sin later. Did he tell you when he wants to do this?"

"Tomorrow night. He wants to take me to his courtroom tomorrow afternoon to explain his process." I am trying my very best to be okay sitting here talking about it.

Tomorrow I'm going to watch St John kill someone.

Rose's attitude is helping. Watching her switch between hardened and compassionate makes me feel better, like I can learn to handle this, like this is what we do. She makes it feel unpleasant but necessary, like the whole business is wrapped around with checks and balances.

"He may need something afterward," she says.

I look inquiringly at her. "What like a drink or something?"

How I must weary her because she rubs her eyes again. "No, Natalie, like a prostitute, sometimes a dominant. He has a pain fetish; sometimes he wants to give it, sometimes he needs to feel it. He'll let you know what he wants and which gender."

I try to keep my face neutral, l but I feel the facade of normal crumbling. I was meant to be a policy gal. I was going to work on shoring up those checks and balances. I was going to lobby for the department, lobby for the program, make sure my sister got a better than even chance of a life. Now I see just how convoluted the road ahead will be. To get to where I want to be, first I have to watch people die, and then I'm going to procure sex workers for my instrument as a reward.

I shrug and shake my head. "I don't know, ma'am, I'm starting to feel a bit out of my depth here. I just don't think I am going to be any good at this."

For some reason, my eyes are stinging.

Less than twenty-four hours in, two meetings with St John, two videos of random deaths, an appointment to watch an execution, and it's the thought of arranging for Sin to fuck someone that tips me over the edge.

I find myself shaking, and I know my jaw is clenched as I try to keep the noises I want to make inside.

"Breathe, Natalie." Rose's voice is softer. "Just breathe. You're going to be fine. You're going to do this."

I look at her and gulp. "I really don't think I am, just so you know."

She gets up and limps around from behind her desk. She's tiny, I keep forgetting that, tiny, elderly, and grey-haired, and her eyes have watched so many people die in a variety of hideous ways.

"If I can do it, you can do it."

I shake my head mutely.

"Okay, pretty girl," her tone is still gentle, "let's go put you back together; I doubt it will be the last time."

She starts to walk towards the door. "Help me on with my coat and lend me your arm. Let's go take a walk outside."

The fresh air revives me. Everything becomes less foggy when I step outside and the nip of autumn in the air slaps my cheeks. Rose huddles in her wool coat, leans on my arm and complains she should have put her winter boots on.

"Come on, let's go sit and look at the trees," she tells me. We make our way across the street to the small park where I sometimes take my sister when they let her out, and she's willing to come. There is a modern sculpture there that she likes. I think it looks like a pretzel in cement, but India is fascinated by it. She says it's like a stick with only one end, which really annoys me because I then have to spend an hour thinking about what that actually means.

India gets into your head that way.

Sort of like Sin.

Rose and I sit on the cold bare bench and look at the flickering flames of leaves on the trees.

"I'm feeling generous today, Natalie, either that or I'm getting old, but either way, I am going to try and help you. Not because I like you, but because I think you would be good for Sin."

I look down at my hands; they aren't shaking currently. They were shaking in the office.

"I was with Sin a long time, too long probably, but I can't be with him forever. Although he hates change, he needs to be challenged in this. He needs to learn that he can establish new connections and go on to live with them. That's important."

She sighs and looks up at the sky which is pale with high clouds. "Sin, as you know, as everyone knows, even though it is barely half the story, was the original student admitted to the program here. They literally built the Early Onset instrument Program around him. The opportunities your little sister has, slim as they are, exist because of Sin.

"He was also the first instrument to have never killed anyone in the wild. He has never, to date, taken a life without legal sanction."

She looks at me seriously. "He is more damaged than you can possibly imagine. He has endured things that are impossible to comprehend. He is short-tempered, has a pain fetish, would kill you in an instant if he thought he could get away with it, but he is also brave, honest, and surprisingly kind to those who need it most.

"He would deny a lot of those things, but I have been with him from the beginning, and I too am honest."

"What happened to him?" I ask. "There are all these rumours about him being super dangerous, but nobody knows where he came from."

"Oh, no, pretty lady, you have to earn more information, and it will have to be from him. I'm not giving you the keys to all the locks."

"I genuinely don't know if I can do this, Rose."

"You can, Natalie, and you will. You actually need to, because if you don't understand and empathize with what goes on in the field, you can never hope to advocate on behalf of people like your sister.

"I know you want to be charming them in the seats of power, but you need more mileage on you first, honey, or you won't convince anyone that things can be different."

"I'm not convincing anyone now. I think my charm fell out of my ass the minute St John walked into the room!"

She laughs, natural and loud, and a smile tugs at my lips. She slaps my thigh. "It'll come back, pretty girl, it's too ingrained. You're just a little shocked at the moment."

We sit and watch the trees for a little longer until I eventually pull myself together. "So how does it work then, after the event?"

"I'll send you a list of names," she says. "He'll let you know if he needs someone after the execution. I have male and female sex workers and a professional dominant you can call. He won't use euphemisms; he'll be straight with you."

I nod reluctantly. Somehow the idea still makes me tense.

"After an execution, he is difficult. It turns him on, and that arousal comes out in all sorts of ways. He'll try to test you, push you, rile you, but you have got to stay calm and let him get it out of his system."

I nod again; this job is killing my language skills.

"I'll see you after the event, just for a debrief." I'm grateful that she is trying to reassure me. "But I know you've got this, you know the protocols inside out. You are trained, Natalie, you are competent, and you were top of your class."

"I got this." I try to sound confident.

She pats my leg again, and I think that maybe I do have a little charm left because I thought she despised me earlier.

She must be a mind reader because she says. "Don't think I'm going soft on you; I've just spent a lot of years on that boy. I want the best for him, and you are the best."

After escorting Rose back to her office, I stop off at the Early Onset Unit before heading back to my condo. I have a special pass that I charmed out of the tutors years ago. It lets me in without going through security. The unit is locked up like a national treasure or an anthrax sample.

I peek in through the wide glass window of India's study room. She's got her back to the window, working at a bench, her skinny body with its shapeless haircut hunched over a microscope. She's wearing jeans she is growing out of and a rainbow coloured t-shirt. Angela, her tutor, sees me lurking at the edge of the window, she shakes her head, the smallest of motions, and I back away quietly.

It seems India is having a bad day, so I'll stay out her way.

My phone vibrates in my pocket.

How about you take her out for lunch in a couple of days? She should be in a better mood by then. Sry, today isn't a good one.

I texted a quick reply to Angela. *Tks, let me know when. Tell her we can do a sushi train, see if that motivates her.*

I get a thumbs-up response a couple of seconds later.

Now all I have to do is kill time until tomorrow afternoon when St John will take me to his courtroom.

I am so brainwashed. I used the euphemistic language of the department without thinking. Tomorrow I get to have a killer show off his killing room to me, complete with instruments of torture.

God, I wish I didn't find him so attractive. Still, tomorrow will likely be the kiss of death on that burgeoning crush.

Chapter Three

St John

"How are you?" only Rose can ask me that question and have a hope of getting an answer, but then she has been asking it for a long time.

When I was younger, I didn't understand the question at all, which frustrated me, but I have learned how she means it over the years.

"I'm edgy. I was frustrated at the delay, and the new steward is a surprise. That is unsettling me."

"How is she a surprise?"

Because we have known each other for so long, I can actually answer the question without concern that it will be misunderstood or used against me.

"I don't know if I want to fuck her or kill her."

"Why stop at one?"

"Now, I know you are being snarky," I growl at her, and she laughs.

Rose is the closest thing I have ever found to someone who understands me. Not that it was easy, it took twenty years, and I am pretty sure she had to rebuild her whole personality to do it because I certainly couldn't.

"She is very pretty," she agrees with me.

"Did you get her as a present for me?" I ask, and I'm not really teasing.

"I guess we'll have to see. Just don't unwrap her and break her straight away, okay?"

I genuinely laugh at that.

"I've signed off on the kill," Rose says. We never bother with diplomatic jargon when we speak to each other. "It's a shame that there was an additional murder while we waited for your steward."

"It irritated me, but the circumstances didn't warrant a kill without sanction."

"You don't like this one do you?"

"I have no respect for him; he's not worthy of any."

"Yes, I thought he was particularly sloppy in the video. Makes me want to send you after the Police Commissioner for allowing his officers to be so blind."

I hum in agreement. That would be more challenging, finding enough evidence amongst the corridors of power to justify my type of punishment. I wish they would let us loose on politicians. We could make the people's choices so much easier.

"You will take him tomorrow night?"

"That's my plan." I toy with my paintbrush. I am illuminating a passage from the Iliad - I find illuminating manuscripts a calming hobby. I'm at the fun part, colouring in the monsters. I place the phone on the side of the lectern I use for this and switch it to speaker so I can paint a centaur's tail in gold.

"Natalie will find tomorrow difficult." Rose's voice is clearer without me holding the phone awkwardly against my ear.

"Will she?"

"You know she will. Despite her training, and her sister, it will still be her first real experience."

"You expect me to modify it for her?"

"God, no."

Which is just as well, because I won't change a thing.

"She will have to take her baptism of fire like we all do," I say, concentrating on the delicate curls of the centaur's tail - centaurs are so sexy, all that manly torso and brute animal strength. They are my favourite monsters.

"Feeling a little biblical tonight?"

"Fuck, no!" I dip the single strand brush into the liquid gold and stroke it across the velum. "Does this conversation have any further purpose, Rose? I'm busy."

A sigh breathes down the phone. "Trust me, Sin, she is the right steward for you, but as I said, don't break her."

"Okay," I mutter reluctantly.

"Goodnight, darling," she says.

I remember her tucking me into a soft bed when my back was stiff and aching, and I didn't understand the endearment back then. I kept telling her my name wasn't *darling*.

"Goodnight."

Silence descends on my office. There is just light pooling around me, the gold paint I now use to fill in the centaur's hooves, and the smooth, hard, wood of the lectern beneath my forearms. I wonder how Natalie will react tomorrow.

I realize I am interested, really interested, to see it.

Natalie

We study a lot about an instrument's courtroom when they are training us to be Stewards. Each courtroom is unique to its Hander; it's their territory, their home ground, generally where they are most comfortable, and it's an intensely personal space for them. We are told it is a reflection of their personality and their deviancy.

Under the law, once guilt has been ascertained, the instrument is responsible for collecting the guilty, transporting them to their courtroom, then delivering and enacting the sentence. The sentence is always death; only the method is variable.

The form of execution is dependent on the crime, and while a steward will often assist an instrument with investigations and has the ultimate duty to sign off on guilt, once within the courtroom, all the steward can do is watch. The instrument runs the show.

I am fucking scared to death of what this day will bring.

When I woke up this morning, it was in a cold sweat.

By the time I am outside the building waiting for St John, I am damn near sick with nerves.

Getting into his innocuous silver SUV feels like the stupidest thing I have ever done.

Who gets into a car with a killer and merrily drives off to the place where they kill people?

All the drama in my head feels like an overreaction when we head out of the city into the pretty landscape of Maryland, and onto the leaf peeping turnpikes of late autumn.

St John's courtroom isn't in the city.

I can see his faint smile when I glance sideways at him, but he says nothing, just deftly manoeuvres the vehicle onto smaller and smaller roads, with less and less traffic until, about forty minutes from the city, he turns into a gated driveway.

The gates are high, solid and anything but ornamental, just flat metal plate, locked with a chain and padlock. They give no hint as to what is behind them.

We're a couple of miles from the nearest town, and when St John opens the car door I hear only the sound of the wind in the trees, rustling the last dry leaves.

He unlocks the gates and pushes them open.

"Welcome to Anathema," he says when he gets back into the car and drives through the entrance.

"Anathema?"

"It's the family name for the place, always has been."

I don't know what I expected to be behind the gate, a junkyard, a wilderness of scrub, a shipping container turned into a torture chamber - every cliché out of the killer hiding in plain sight playbook. I didn't expect a sweeping drive, lofty trees, and a view across meadowland to the wide waters of the Potomac, sparkling in the fall sunshine.

It is peaceful and innocent at first glance, almost like Sin himself, but the details make it clear that this is no ordinary place.

Sin stops the car again and gets out to close the gates behind us.

The driveway is well-maintained paving, with a light dusting of fallen leaves. Further down the drive, looking upriver, a large house stands roofless, the blank eyes of its windows bleeding sooty streaks like running mascara.

St John gets back into the car, and we drive past it. "The old family home," he says. I eye the burned-out ruin and wait for further information that doesn't come.

The driveway swings in a graceful curve to the right. I lose sight of the river as we enter a grove of trees, silver-barked and yellow-leaved, their narrow trunks rise up from long grass.

A building, covered in creepers that have already turned appropriately blood-red, comes into view. One and half stories with a low, flared roofline and wide brick arched windows, it survived the fire that ravaged the main house, even though some of the windows are boarded up.

St John parks beside the building, and we climb out onto a gravel path. The air smells of damp leaves, and there is no sound apart from the trees whispering to each other.

It is surprisingly peaceful and beautiful.

"Come on." St John isn't explaining anything, but I'm here to learn, and I just need to wait and see.

St John unlocks a robust, modern-looking door in the old Flemish bond brick and leads me inside.

I am immediately struck by a sense of space and the smell of wood and dust. The feeling of age is highlighted by the scattering of sunbeams that nudge past the creepers that try to smother the sash windows that still have glass in them.

St John flicks a panel beside the door. Lights come on, fluorescents that flicker into life and flood the room, bringing out the details. Most of the space is high and open, clear up to the roof beams. The wood of the joists is black with age, but I can see the tiny noggins and the chisel marks around the hand-cut joints. A wide arched doorway to the outside has been boarded up securely, and an open mezzanine level, that once must have been a loft, covers a third of the floor space.

"Wow," I say quietly.

"This was the carriage house," Sin says, and he seems almost embarrassed for some reason.

"It's an extraordinary building."

"Yes, it's the only complete building left on the estate now." He says estate like that's a normal thing to have.

Sin leads me across the brick floor towards the back of the carriage house. The space isn't empty, but it isn't cluttered either; there are some old tools hanging rusty on the bare brick walls, a saddle rack that could have taken ten but now has only one small lonely English saddle on it, its leather dull and cracked. There are a few sacks in a corner and a mismatched collection of earthenware pottery on a shelf.

Where the stalls for the horses would have been, beneath the mezzanine, a black wall runs the width of the building with a single door in it.

"This is my courtroom."

The door is not innocuous, it's steel and heavy. While it's not screaming 'portal of doom' it's very clear that whatever is on the other side is serious shit.

"Okay," I say.

"I need to make something very clear."

I wait, I have learned that St John isn't keen on pointless affirmatives.

"This room is custom-built, it's hard to get into, it only opens to my palm print, and it's even harder to get out. The intention is that three of us will enter this room, and the two that leave alive are you and me. That is the intention, not a guarantee."

I stay silent. I know this, it's drummed into us over the course of training, and we sign away all rights to sue for reckless endangerment, but if St John wants to give the lecture, he can. This is his courtroom.

He pushes open the door, and I step through first.

The lights come on as soon as the door opens. Roughly thirty-feet square, the room's floor is gloss black and seamless, there is a surgical type table on castors in the middle of the room, its single central leg houses hydraulics and its control box hangs from a hook on the side. A rolling stool sits next to it. It's hard to ignore the full set of restraints fitted to it.

Along one wall is an array of wall and floor cabinets with a stainless steel countertop and a sluice sink. Three basic and solid-looking chairs are lined up next to each other along another wall.

The light source is invisible, which is the only thing that differentiates it from an operating room. It even smells faintly of disinfectant.

"Clean," I say because I can't think of anything else.

This seems to please Sin, who seems proud of that assessment.

"The exact layout varies depending on the circumstances. I change it depending on what the kill demands. I won't be using the surgical bed for our current case, this won't be a complex or lengthy execution, and I would prefer him sitting."

He pulls a second rolling stool from behind the door and pushes it towards me. "Sit. This next bit is important."

Gingerly, I lower myself onto the stool. St John remains standing. He is so in his element here. This is his domain, he designed it, and he rules it. Everything in here is just as he wants - give or take the rules they lay down around us.

"For your safety, there is a gun taped to the underneath of the counter, here." He indicates the end of the cabinet to my right. "The gun is loaded. I will have checked it before the execution.

"There is also a button that will, in a dire emergency, release a fast-acting, highly effective aerosol agent that is a derivative of 3-methylfen-tanyl." He shows me a panel set into the interior of the entrance door frame at waist height. It has to be pressed in and down to reveal the button. "The intention is that if it is released the gas will take us all down. When it is triggered, this room locks down and headquarters is informed.

"That button is an option of last resort. It's a Hail Mary. The aerosol it releases is highly dangerous, unstable, and requires an antidote. I will also consider it a personal failure if it is ever triggered."

He says *personal failure* in the same way other people say, *punishable by death.*

St John maintains fixed eye contact with me while he goes over these points. His yellow eyes are intense and it's almost impossible to look away. I hang on his every word, my heart rate rising, this time with excitement, not for the execution, but for the adventure it feels like we are in together.

Naturally, St John then ruins the embryonic connection.

"These measures are your only safety net. My job here is not to protect you because you will not be doing anything that requires protection. You will stay back, you will steward, and then file your report. That is the extent of your involvement."

I nod and remind myself that this isn't some game, this is serious fucking work with the worst people alive.

"On the off chance that the client gets the upper hand, you will exit if you can, and leave them here with me."

"Is that likely?" I ask.

"It has happened in the past." This is said in such a way as to make it clear, don't ask about this.

I take the hint.

In here, St John is absolute, resolute, his energy dark and enticing in a way that catches me off guard. I want to obey him because here he is king.

"But what about you?" I ask. It would be hard to turn away and leave my colleague in danger.

He tilts his head and looks blank.

"What if he gets free and kills you?"

"I will be dead."

"Well, yeah, but don't I fight for you?"

"No," he looks annoyed, "you know this."

"Well, yes, theoretically, but I assumed it would be different in the field, everything else damn well is!"

"This is different. The duty is clear. Your only duty is to yourself and I would add that if you are in imminent danger it is because either you, or I, have made a catastrophic mistake." It is clear from his tone that he is sure any mistake will not be his. "Don't ever think about me, if a killer gets the better of me, you must exit without hesitation."

"That feels wrong to me." In a scenario so morally murky, this is where I draw the ethical line? Sometimes I wonder if India is the only certifiable one in our family.

"Why?"

"I don't know, but it feels like we are a team, and I shouldn't leave you if it goes wrong."

"I can assure you I would leave you if necessary."

"Would you? Really?"

"There are angels out there, little steward, but I was never one of them, despite what some people thought. I'm the devil, and I'll certainly take you down with me if the situation calls for it. It's the job. So to be crystal clear, if by some chance you fall along the way I will not come for you, that's a guarantee."

His words hit me like a slap across the face even though they shouldn't.

"Yeah, I get it, but I'm not you. It feels like a dereliction of duty if I leave you, like we should be there for each other."

"You keep talking about feelings like they matter. All I am hearing is '*not ready*' and that makes me irritated."

"No, I am ready. It's just, it's nothing. I'm just verbalising shit."

"As you have done since I met you."

"Okay, understood, no guarantees, three go in, and hopefully, the right two come out."

"Essentially, yes."

"Okay."

St John shows me the rest of his courtroom. There is a small shower room slash storage room for cleaning products off the main room. Access is via a coded panel. The cabinets contain a nauseating variety of cutting tools as well as more archaic implements, ropes, and the garrotte St John will use tonight.

I find myself getting a little lightheaded, not because I'm squeamish, but I think I just need some fresh air.

St John obviously senses my need for a break and guides me outside, engaging the lock on his courtroom behind him.

I breathe easier once we leave the sterile but creepy courtroom - the black floor, the illuminated ceiling, it all adds to the feeling of otherworldliness. Stepping back into the wood fragrant, slowly crumbling, gently ageing interior of the carriage house is like moving between dimensions.

I make my way over to the entrance and open it. "Do you mind if I look around outside?"

He shrugs. "Knock yourself out. We'll be here a lot and there are sixteen acres to explore. Go take a walk, get the lay of the land."

Trees surround the carriage house. Their falling leaves have rolled a gold carpet down the gravel path that I follow towards the ruins of the main house.

Follow the yellow brick road.

The land slopes steeply from the house to the river, and the burned-out ruins of St John's family home are sad and jagged, but I can see the elegant lines it once had.

"There was a terrace." I didn't hear Sin come up behind me, his footfalls silent on the damp ground. "It wrapped around the whole building. My nanny used to let me eat breakfast out there in the summer."

"How did it burn down?"

"I burned it."

"Oh." Every conversation I seem to have with Sin gets derailed by the bombs he drops into them. I don't think he does it on purpose, he's just very blunt and honest.

We walk slowly around the perimeter of the house. I can see the carved ornamental edges of the windows and doorways, and the tall narrow chimneys that rise above the gaping hole of the roof seem to touch the sky.

"It must have been quite the place in its day," I say eventually.

St John nods. "My family have owned this estate for nearly three hundred years, it had a lot of time to bed into the landscape." His shoulders are hunched, his body language more defensive than I have seen before. "There was a boxwood garden behind the house where my mother walked with the men who admired her. She hosted parties in the garden in the summer, with a string quartet in the summer house that was over there." He nods towards a little rise above the river, now just flat stones beside a tall shading tree.

"Sounds idyllic."

"Not really." He jerks his head, and I follow him.

The grass is longer behind the house. The box garden ruins are sad and overgrown. The elderly shrubs are gnarled, straggling, and dying from beneath. Sin leads me past the garden towards the leaning remains of a white picket fence, now scabbed with grey and green lichen, which forms a square enclosure under dark evergreens.

He puts his hands in his pockets. "One of my early playgrounds."

I lean over the fence and see it is a family graveyard, the stones laid flat in the grass, their etched names ranging in clarity, some blurred, some crisp. I step closer but not beyond the entrance. I don't feel like stepping on Sin's hallowed ground.

It takes a little while to notice but then it is obvious, so many of the names on the gravestones are the same, St John Morton Miller.

I turn and look at Sin, he shrugs. "Family tradition. Every generation there is me."

"You grew up playing around graves that had your name on them?"

"Oh, we've been seriously fucked up for generations. I'm just the ultimate expression!"

"Never ceases to amaze me," I say, "Parents, normally the foundation of every problem!"

We walk slowly back to the carriage house. Sin is less scary out here in the sunshine, the light catches little gold strands in his dark hair, and his eyes seem more pale green than yellow. I can see the dark ring around the irises and his cheeks are a little flushed from the cold breeze off the river.

His hands are deep in the pockets of his black combats and his short black jacket has the collar turned up.

I wonder if he feels the generations that came before him when he walks on his land.

"So why do you call it Anathema?" I ask.

"It's always been called that. It was built on a small piece of land my family acquired after the main farm. Originally it was a community of Christians, a breakaway sect, a cult I suppose. They were massacred by their neighbours one day when word got out about how they chose to conduct themselves. Forty men, women and children died. Apparently how they chose to worship was considered anathema. My family kept the name."

"That's horrible."

"It was several hundred years ago, but yeah, we're a horrible family. It was also my father's favourite nickname for me."

I stare at him, lost for words. "Your family gets more charming by the minute."

"Just don't start feeling sorry for me, newbie. It's all a nasty story, and you haven't heard the half of it yet, but I was born this way."

"Am I allowed to ask about your nasty story?"

"Don't expect an answer; I don't know you well enough."

I nudge his shoulder with mine. "I'm going to be your next best friend."

He shakes his head in amazement. "You are either the bravest, or the stupidest, steward I ever met. And we don't even know if you're going to make it through the night yet."

That brings me back with a bump. When he showed me the graves that shared his name and told me about the horrible nickname, I felt sorry for him. For a moment, I forgot why we were here, and what comes next.

That was the thing with Sin, he made me forget myself. I drift into treating him like any other man I find attractive, and then he reminds me he is feral, primal, and to be feared.

When we reach the carriage house, St John leans against the side of the SUV. "Did Rose mention my fetish to you?" He looks me straight in the eye; there's no sign of embarrassment, no shame.

I nod and feel the beginnings of a blush on my cheeks.

Maybe being like St John wouldn't be so bad. I struggled a lot with my sexuality as a teen, but I'm cool with it now. I find it awesome that I'm attracted to people not genders, but I still have a long way to go when it comes to kinks. I had never been brave enough to explore the things that in my head turned me on.

St John got to be open about his desires; that must feel amazing.

"So you know pain is my thing?"

"Yes, Rose mentioned that you might need something and that you would tell me what you wanted."

"Judging by your blushes, this is another thing that didn't get mentioned much during training."

I shrug. "Training was a lot of legal stuff. I guess they thought we would work out the kinks in the field."

He rolls his eyes at my pathetic pun. "There has to be a payoff for the Instruments or there is no motivation for them to keep doing this legally. Some insist on little trophies, some like time alone with the body afterward."

I can't hide my revulsion at that.

"Don't be naive, Natalie," he admonishes. "But maybe count yourself lucky that I'm just straight up kinky."

"You get aroused by pain?" My tongue feels thick in my mouth when I say the word aroused, and god help me, I feel my nipples tingle and tighten. I pull my coat around me more securely, hiding my interest.

"Yes, I get off on pain; it excites me."

I keep my face as blank as possible, but I can't help the way my gaze flickers to his crotch, to where his combats stretch tight across his bulge, which is all too obvious from his position leaning against the side of the car.

Of course, he notices. A small smile plays across his lips, but he says nothing.

"Is that why you need relief afterward? Because of the pain fetish?"

"Yes, but I'm complicated. I don't just get off on their pain; I get off on mine too." He taps his head. "Wired wrong. I work both ways; all pain makes me hard."

I force myself to keep my eyes above his waist.

"And you're bisexual too?"

"Yes. You could say execution is a no-loss situation for me. If they get loose, I get pain. If they don't get loose, they get pain. If it's men or if it's women I still get turned on. Win-win as far as my deviancies are concerned."

"Is there any particular reason you're telling me this, other than trying to make me embarrassed?"

He grins. "While making you embarrassed is actually both fascinating and easy, I'm telling you because you need to understand that pain isn't something I fear; it's something I welcome. You appeared worried about me earlier, about what you should do if things go wrong. Well, one thing you don't need to do is worry about is me suffering; I'd enjoy it. I was just trying to reassure you."

"Talking about your immediate sexual response to painful stimuli isn't hugely reassuring."

"Hey, at least I'm not lapping at their blood, or jerking off over their corpses, or talking them to death like some of my colleagues. I kill them, I get excited, and I get my release afterward."

I nod. "Getting that loud and clear. Do I need to line up anyone for tonight?" I make a point of looking down at his crotch now; the dig about my embarrassment bugging me.

"I won't know what I want until it's done. I'll let you know."

"Okay." I don't want to make eye contact with him. I'm struggling anyway, and this just makes it more difficult. "If you need it tonight, where do you want it? Here?"

"No, back in the city. Nobody comes in here but you and me."

I nod again. They really need to stress this part of the job during training, but maybe they don't know. When I finish this fieldwork stint, I'm going to rewrite the whole fucking course from a nice warm office.

"Anything else I need to know about tonight?" I ask, keen for a change of topic, not least because my body has been stirring in response to Sin.

"Tonight is shakedown. Don't expect efficiency tonight. We're both going to be playing it by ear. It's likely to get messy. Just stand back and keep breathing."

Again, not so much with the reassurance, but at least he is being honest.

"Thanks," I say, and I find I mean it.

As we get into the car, I look around and shake my head. "I never thought your courtroom would be somewhere like this. This place is beautiful; it feels weird to still be able to see that knowing what happens here."

St John looks around as if seeing it for the first time. "I guess so. It's hard for me to see it like others do because I was born here."

"It holds bad memories for you? That's why you use it for this?"

"Nobody has ever asked me that before. It just seemed a logical place to me. My childhood was not happy, but I don't blame the place for that."

"But you burned your family home down," I point out.

He starts the car but sits quietly, frowning, thinking. He appears to be genuinely trying to explain himself to me. I take heart that we're both trying to find a way to communicate. "I wasn't punishing this place when I burned the house down. I wasn't trying to destroy it. I think it was symbolic, by burning it down, the person I was born as ceased to exist. I think I was wiping the slate clean, becoming the instrument."

"How did that feel?"

He turns and looks at me. I see the tiger again, burning bright. "Now that, Natalie, is a really stupid question because I don't feel anything. I'm not capable of it."

"Other than pain."

"Other than pain," he agrees, "and pain is good."

Chapter Four

St John

I can hear Natalie in my ear. She keeps asking if I am ok. I keep ignoring her.

I like the night. It's my peaceful place, where I walk in the shadows and don't have to pretend - all that posturing they taught me growing up, how to look normal. In the night, I am just me, and I'm utterly confident that I'm the nastiest thing out here.

"St John, St John, can you hear me?" Natalie will need additional coaching in coms protocol. I imagine holding her head underwater and only letting her up to whisper in her ear, "Don't make pointless noises."

I must have muttered that aloud because I hear her huff and grumble, "Could have just said *Roger* the first time I asked."

I find a smile tugging at my lips. Either I'm looking forward to a kill, or the idea of Natalie suffering really does appeal to me.

Following the tree shadows, I glide through the park. The night is cold, the first real cold night of winter coming in, baring its teeth. The red maples out on the estate will be appropriately bloody in a few days. The sugar maples by the carriage house are already flaming gold as the days shorten.

The majority of the destitute have begged places in the homeless shelters tonight or are huddled over the steamy gratings of well-lit sidewalks. Only the drunk and the deranged will voluntarily choose the park tonight.

Cawston came early to the park tonight. He has already jogged the trail three times looking for a victim while I watch from the edges of the well-lit world. He must be feeling greedy and desperate tonight; maybe some smug husband of a trophy wife made him feel less than successful. Who knows?

All I know is that he normally does two circuits, and if nothing prey-shaped arrives, he goes home and jerks off to strangulation porn.

I think he will go for a man tonight, he needs to kill a man to feel like a man – what stupid reasoning.

Cawston is coming to the end of his third lap when a suitable victim appears, or rather staggers into view. He's too drunk to feel the cold and bitterly berating the state of the world, muttering to himself as he tongue kisses a bottle in a brown paper bag.

Spotting him from a distance, Cawston steps into the shadows himself and goes into hunter mode.

I have to admit, I like taking them when they think they are about to kill. Stopping them at the climax is a foible of mine - let's call it edging for killers.

I could just as easily have taken Cawston in his home as he tied his shoelaces, on the street as he brought a takeout home, or before he ever completed one circuit of the park, but I like to do it this way, and I am allowed.

Lawyers in their courtrooms operate within an adversarial system. Instruments in the wild do the same, but with less safeguards in place.

We take our prisoners without warrants, fanfare, or audience. We take them where they stand, in secret, preferably in silence. It adds to our mystique and the fear our existence generates.

Natalie is still muttering in my ear as I drift, slow as a falling leaf, through the deeper dark of the wooded area towards where Cawston lurks, using the body of a sturdy dogwood to mask his shape.

He will wait for the drunk to pass him and then step up behind him, efficient but boring.

The tension within me vibrates.

Grumbling to himself, the drunk moves down the path. I can smell the sharp acid of cheap liquor above the thick organic body odour that wafts from him in the cold night air. Funny how my senses go into over-drive at times like this; I can almost taste him.

Natalie is nervously tapping something hard against the dashboard of the car. It pulls me from my reverie, reminds me I am a man on a mission, not an animal about to taste prey. If it's a pen, I'm going to stab her in the thigh with it later, but it's a timely interruption, or I'll watch, entranced, as another murder is committed.

I slide around behind Cawston; his stupid running shoes are bright blobs of colour even in the greying of the night. He is easy to see as he waits in place. The drunk rambles past, oblivious. Cawston reaches into his pocket for his garrotte.

With a single step, I close on him. Wrapping my arm around his neck, I grasp his jaw, twisting his head to the side. Using my weight, I pin him against the tree.

"Move and I snap it," I whisper into his ear. He freezes because no killer expects an interruption when their attention is on their victim and arousal is thrumming.

With my right hand, I press into the side of his neck, feeling for the carotid.

I trained a thousand times a thousand to get this right, fast and accurate.

I feel the ribbon of oxygen-rich blood pulsing deep in the tissue. I slide the needle home and depress the plunger, pumping etorphine directly into his bloodstream.

He jerks at the needle sting, but I hold him tight and let biology work as I count down the seconds until he is out.

"Collection in three," I say aloud as Cawston's weight in my grip steadily increases as he goes limp.

I continue counting in my head. This stuff isn't instantaneous, and I don't get the opportunity to check that I've hit the carotid, but I've done it enough to be confident that I did, and Cawston isn't playing possum as he sags.

"Roger that." Natalie is brisk now, business-like. I hope she stays that way. It is very different having him in my head instead of Rose.

I give Cawston a full two minutes. One minute should be enough, but I'd rather err on the side of caution.

I keep him pinned to the tree as I wait, and I watch the old drunk carry on down the pathway, oblivious, anesthetized in his own way.

I have this down to a fine art now, I've been doing it for years. Rose, for all her qualities, never played any part in the logistics of execution. While she was always in my ear during collection when it came to transporting the body into my courtroom, she kept out of the way, going through her private mental preparation.

Natalie doesn't have procedures yet, and she hovers around me trying to be helpful when I manoeuvre Cawston from the SUV to the trolley I use to roll him into the courtroom.

I can feel her emotional state. It needles at me, a prickling mix of dread and excitement. Eventually, I tell her to fuck off and wait until I call her into the room.

She goes reluctantly, and paces the brick floor of the carriage house while I prepare Cawston.

I secure Cawston to a plain wooden chair in the middle of the room. I expect him to struggle and try to escape. It's part of my deliberate cruelty to allow him wiggle room within the wrist bonds. It's why I choose rope instead of the more reliable cable ties.

Inside me, the killer I keep barely under control paces restlessly, eager to get to work, ready to play. His desire causes him to snarl and rush the bars of the cage I keep him inside.

I shiver with desire and tighten the muscles in my pelvis, feeling the pleasure tingle at the root of my cock. Rotating my neck, I force my shoulders to drop and relax. I breathe deeply a few times, find my center, mentally slowing myself down, denying myself the urge to rush this.

I dim the lights in the room until there is just a central spotlight on Cawston then I call Natalie in.

When I say her name, she spins towards me. From the angle of her head and the jerk of tension in her body, she's already pumped with adrenaline. If I had more sense and less confidence, I would calm her first, but the burn of energy in her system finds its mate in mine, and I'm too close now.

Come with me, little steward; let's see who you really are.

"Sit," I say to Natalie as I close the door behind her. In the dim light at the edges of the room, her eyes are bright, her cheeks flushed. She licks her lips and lowers herself onto the rolling stool, then pushes back until her back is against the door.

"Remember the rules," my voice is tight with excitement, "and stick to your role. You are here to steward."

Her breathing is rapid and her nostrils flare with the air her body demands she pull in. I give her a predatory smile. I want to kiss her and taste what she is feeling. It would be so fresh and new.

Natalie's emotional state is as much a reflection of my dominance as the situation she finds herself in.

She is responding to me, the real me, killer me, and that's delicious. It's the salt in the meal - better in than on - it's the lime in the beer - keep the flies away - it's the erection in the confessional - look at me being all taboo.

I spin away from her, tempted beyond belief, and retreat to the deeper shadows behind Cawston, to wait for him to stir.

Natalie

Cawston is stirring, and I'm frozen in place directly in his line of sight.

My back is to the proverbial wall, and St John, wrapped in his mantle of predator, waits in the shadows behind the man tied to the chair.

Cawston's head has fallen forward on his chest. His arms are behind his back, tied to the wooden chair. I did expect more elaborate restraints, but this is how St John views Cawston, pretty damn basic.

Cawston coughs weakly and lifts his head. He lost his beanie in the SUV, and his shoulder-length hair hangs over his face. He shakes his head, flicking his hair out of his eyes and catches sight of me. His eyes narrow. An almost hysterical part of me wants to give him a little wave.

"Do you know where you are?" St John's voice comes out of the dark, low and steady.

"No." Cawston shakes his head again, his movements jerky. He spits on the floor. I guess his mouth tastes vile after the drug.

"I am an instrument. You are in my Courtroom. The steward is present."

His head jerks up, eyes wide.

It turns out real fear smells like urine.

"I see you have heard of situations like this." St John sounds amused.

I watch the puddle spread around Cawston's feet; it seems he dresses to the left.

I feel sort of distant, detached, and I recognize the feeling from the lectures. They say that stewarding doesn't feel real at first. It's not stupid remote and unreal like Call of Duty on a screen or anything, but it's definitely detached. It's like I'm not quite present because my brain has decided this is not a reality it's going to accept.

"Whatever this is, man, it's a mistake, you have the wrong guy." Cawston sounds genuine "I don't know what you think I did, but I didn't do it, I'm a personal trainer, man; I just help people get fit."

"I saw you," St John says. "Twice, actually."

There is a pause. Cawston hangs his head.

When he speaks next, he sounds pissed off. "Then why the fuck didn't you stop me?"

Silence.

I have a whole textbook full of answers to that question. Everyone says it is the hardest part of being a steward. Not watching the retribution - our brains often take us out of that because, see above, but the logical question, *why do we have to let killings happen just so we have proof?* That's the one that keeps us awake at night.

I wonder if St John will answer.

The question has jerked me back into reality. I can see St John now, pacing silently just outside the circle of the light. I want to hear his answer too.

No answer comes.

And Cawston laughs, spits again, and shakes his head. "Ah, who gives a fuck? So two more down and outs died with a hard-on, doesn't matter."

"Obviously." St John's voice is silky, not his usual grit. My brain signals danger, danger, because it has experience of Sin now; it knows the voice is angry.

"So what's the plan, Stan?" Cawston tips his head back and shakes his hair out of his eyes. "How does this go down?" He almost sounds giggly now - bless the brain and its drugging cocktail of hormones, re-acting to any given situation.

"Traditionally, I recite the offenses, the steward agrees the sentence, and then I deliver the eye for an eye thing," St John speaks from directly behind Cawston, and the man jerks in his bonds. Not so unafraid then.

"No jury of my peers?" Cawston scrambles for justice.

"I am your peers." St John's voice is harsh now.

"You're not my peer. You kill people who are incapacitated. You're a fucking coward!" Cawston is getting angry. Anger and fear are a heady combination, and his emotions grow thick in the room.

"I am anything but." St John steps fully into the light.

I should be looking at Cawston, but all I can see is St John. He fills my vision, burning bright, and the fact that he comes to kill is doing strange things to my limbic system.

He carries a wire garrotte in his hand. Cawston's eyes zero in on it, mine too, but I'm looking at Sin's hands more than the glinting slithering wire and the polished wood handles. I'm looking at Sin's huge hands and wondering what they would feel like on my body.

St John twirls the garrotte, and I drag my head back into the game. I cannot believe I am responding like this, my body trembling on the verge of arousal, my blood pumping at the sight of Sin in the spotlight. My very own predator, all mine now.

"If I had my way," St John says calmly, "I would starve you for a few days, pour cheap vodka down your throat, inject you with hallucinogens to bring out your worst nightmares, send you stumbling through the streets being ignored by people, and then I would stalk you and kill you. But I'm not allowed to do that. Apparently, that's an *inefficient* use of my time." He actually makes air quotes.

"Who cares, man?" Cawston eyes St John up and down. "Nobody fucking cares; they were just waste. I was cleaning up."

"It's a tough job, but somebody has to do it," St John all but purrs, and Cawston recognizes the insult.

I know that Sin is playing with his food, but that's the trade off. Sin gets to do this until the end, and the end is when he decides, not me. I shift restlessly in the darkness, wondering what will happen next.

St John turns towards me. "I think we can dispense with listing the offenses given Mr Cawston's confession." I feel naked under his burning eyes. "Do you confirm the death sentence, steward?"

I nod.

"I need your words, steward."

I can't refuse St John anything when he uses that imperious tone with me; I am his prisoner as much as Cawston is.

"I confirm the death sentence. You may carry it out." My voice is firmer than I thought it would be, the ritual words falling from my mouth.

"Thank you," says St John formally, but as he turns back towards Cawston it all goes wrong.

I don't know how he did it because Sin's body blocked my view, but Cawston is free and surges to his feet. He grabs the wooden chair, and with all his gym-honed strength, he smashes it into Sin's side.

Sin grunts; the chair splinters as he stumbles. Cawston stabs wildly at Sin with the remains of the chair in his hands. Sin twists to the side, and the sharp end, stake-like, catches him across the ribs. He growls and puts his hand to his side. Cawston, realizing he hasn't succeeded in incapacitating Sin, goes for him with adrenaline-fueled fists. The first punch brings Sin to his knees. The second, delivered by a hysterically laughing Cawston, knocks him face down on the floor.

I don't do what I am supposed to do.

Sin is down.

I don't hold back.

Sin is down.

I leap to his defence and am out of my depth in microseconds because this isn't training, this is real.

The floor is slippery with piss, littered with broken wood, and Cawston is fast and fit. While he's not as well trained as I am, I'm nowhere near as angry as him. I'm mainly scared, and Sin is down.

I don't think I actually land a single blow on Cawston before he swoops and picks up a foot-long length of wood. The ragged end of it is sharp as a broken bone. I can already imagine how it's going to feel when it pierces my skin.

I stumble out of range and edge backward towards where the gun is taped under the counter.

Sin is still down.

"I'm going to gut you, you little bitch." Cawston has the upper hand, I am weaponless. "And then I'm going to ram this up that pissant instrument's ass and watch him bleed out."

I feel my back hit the wall. I'm out of manoeuvring room.

"Look at you, evolving." Sin rises behind Cawston, and the wire of the garrotte is like a flicker of lightning through the air. Cawston's hands reflexively claw at his throat; the wood in his hand stabs his face before he can release it.

Cawston getting free, Sin falling under his attack, everything until now was Sin toying with his prey.

He tests himself, and he tests me.

I failed.

But he still gets to indulge.

I sag against the wall and watch Sin, the professional killer at work.

His face is intent, focussed; he could be listening to choirs in his head, maybe he is. He moves Cawston with the pressure of the wire at his throat, making him dance and sway to the music of the garrotte.

He hasn't even broken a sweat, but I can see the long ragged slice in his shirt and the blood stain that blooms across the fabric.

Sin brings Cawston to his knees and plants a knee in his back, between his shoulder blades. Cawston has no voice; the wire has taken it. He grips that torturing strand with his bare hands, and I can't see his face because of the hair falling over it. I see the frantic jerking of his muscles though and sense his pain mushrooming through his body, hands and throat, brain and spine.

"You really should have run when you had the chance. Running would have been sensible." Sin meets my gaze over Cawston's head. "My cases often get free. I like to see what they will do. None of them has ever tried to escape. They always try for one more kill."

Sin's eyes glow yellow like tourmaline, like the eyes of an idol our ancestors would sacrifice to. There is now something implacable in his face. Something greedy and fierce bathes in the pain that radiates from Cawston and fills the room.

Sin is like some warrior angel, and he is beautiful.

"You have made many bad choices; that was the last one." His hands twist, the muscles in his shoulders flex, and his knee pushes into Cawston's back. It presses him beyond his physical limits, beyond life. I think I feel his soul let go, like an elastic snap, or maybe that was his neck.

There is a gush of blood, a gulping sound, and then Sin flicks the garrotte free.

Cawston slumps to the floor.

Sin looks at me. The predator isn't satisfied yet; he's just getting started.

Chapter Five

Natalie

"Now it's your turn," Sin says. I would do anything for him at this point because he saved me, because he damns me, because he is something otherworldly. I want him to want me, and I'm so fucking scared.

"He hurt you!" It's the only reason I have, and I need him to know that.

Sin's hand presses to his ribs and blood seeps between his fingers like a slow red tide. It isn't the only blood on his hands and for some reason I find the glisten of it pretty.

Cawston is on the floor, his head at an impossible angle. His throat is a ragged red mess where Sin's wire was and then wasn't.

I drag my eyes from Sin's ribs to his face. The rage in them flays me. "What the fuck did you think you were doing?" Sin's voice is always low, but now it grates.

"You were down."

"Temporarily. He wouldn't have won. I am infinitely superior."

"But..." I don't get to finish the sentence before he is right up in my space.

I watch as Sin digs his fingers into the slice of the cut across his ribs, and he goes white around the lips from the pain. It hits me that pain turns him on. I glance down and see the bulge in his pants. Without thinking, I lick my lips.

His hand clamps around my throat, and he pins me against the wall. "Open up."

I stare at him, confused.

"Open your fucking mouth."

I cannot take my eyes off him, but I slowly open my mouth.

He lifts his bloody hand towards my face and forces three fingers into my mouth. I gag at the copper thick taste, but he presses further in.

"I am going to fuck your mouth, and it's going to be deeper than this."

His face is so close to mine, three of his fingers are down my throat, he has blood on his lips, I have blood in my mouth, and my breath is in his hands.

"I have to teach you somehow, Natalie, looks like you choose this way."

I have never been so turned on in my life.

He rips his fingers out of my mouth and kisses me like he wants to kill me, which he probably does. I can't help it, I don't just let him, I kiss him back. I push the taste of blood back into his mouth, and he sucks on my tongue, growling softly. His hand around my throat tightens, and I reach up to grab his forearm.

He releases my throat, grabs a handful of my hair, twisting it around his fist. "Knees, now."

I don't fold, I drop, my knees hitting the hard black floor with an audible crack.

I am kneeling in blood, and Sin, one handed, is freeing his cock from his pants.

Swaying back and forth, I can hardly wait.

His hand is in my hair tugs my head back. "Open your mouth."

Opening my mouth for him is the most natural thing in the world now. He spits in my mouth. I want him to do it again.

I plead with my eyes. *Please more.*

I can smell the blood, the blood on my face, the blood he has twisted into my hair, the blood that drips in slow rivulets down his side towards the hand that holds his cock.

He holds my head back further, I guess he wants the right angle. He feeds his cock into my mouth and my eyes must roll back into my head because it never felt like this before.

His cock is thick, musky, relentless, as it forces its way in, and I gag around it, my head jerking, my chest tightening, but he doesn't stop, he just keeps going and I feel the fat head of it press into the sensitive places of my throat. He groans and leans forward to rest a forearm against the wall and his forehead on his arm so he can look down on me.

I am forced to look up at him, eyes streaming, throat convulsing. He starts to fuck my mouth and he tells me why.

"You got wet over what I did. I saw it in your eyes. Fear turns you on."

I try to shake my head, but his hand holds my hair too tight. All I can do is groan and drool around the cock that fills my mouth and drives the taste of his bloody fingers deep into my throat.

This is not me, this was never me, until suddenly it is, and I've become more me in moments than I did in decades.

I flex my hips, my clit throbbing. I tighten my muscles, trying to give myself some semblance of relief from the flood of arousal. I scrabble at the button of my combats, I need to touch myself, I have to.

"I could fuck you over that dead body, and you would thank me for it."

My pants are open and I'm forcing my hand down inside my panties, my fingertips aiming for the hot sensitive centre of me. I pinch my clit between my fingers and groan around Sin's cock at the surge of pleasure.

The eyes glaring down at me glow with a predatory gleam; I'm transfixed by them. He smiles, holds me against his groin, the root of his cock stretching my lips, snot and tears pulse from me.

When he pulls me off, I'm ragdoll limp, panting. Black spots dance in front of my eyes, but my hand is still in my panties.

"Once more, take it one more time."

I nod imperceptibly, ashamed. He laughs, then dribbles thick spit down onto my filthy face. I try to catch it on my tongue.

He tilts his hips and offers his cock to me. I open my mouth willingly, and he slides in again. I breathe in through my nose, tilt my head back, and let him have me. I am a hole he can use, and it feels amazing.

I am floating.

He pulls out and I pant quietly, my fingers pinching at my clit as roughly as he is using my mouth, my knees sore on the floor.

His hand in my hair pulls me up. I struggle to my feet, slumping back against the wall.

"What a pretty mess you are."

I look at him through drugged eyes, and he leans in and licks the side of my cheek.

"Little spot there," he says, and laughs at me.

"Please." I'm not sure what I am asking for. Somehow, I just trust him to know.

He pins his forearm against my much-abused throat. "How close are you?"

"I don't think we've ever been closer." My voice is wrecked as I look down at how we are pressed together.

"Still making with the smart remarks, even at this stage." He presses against my throat, and I sob for him. "You don't come until I do, you're lucky I'm going to let you touch yourself."

He pushes me back down and my mouth is already open as my knees slam into the floor. He hisses and pumps his hips, his cock doing deep into my throat while I tap my clit. I'm holding onto my orgasm by the skin of my teeth because I was close even before he gave me a break.

I feel him swelling even more in my mouth, his cock growing noticeably harder as his strokes get shorter, more urgent. I want to fondle his balls, pull at them, drive him over the edge but I can't stop touching myself. It's impossible because I need this so much.

Sin's hips rut forward and my head bangs back against the wall.

I feel his thighs tremble. He moans and I want everything. I want him kissing me, I want him fucking me in every hole I have. I want him to take everything I have to give.

I suck greedily on his cock as he pulls back and his cum spills hot against my tongue, flooding my mouth. I let myself go, and I cum sobbing and trembling as his cock continues to pulse and he holds me up by my hair.

My pussy spasms wildly, my clit feels huge and sharp, and the juice gushing from me is more than I ever remember before.

He lets me go, and still sobbing, I slide down the wall to rest at his feet. There is a dead man behind him, cooling on the floor, and my mouth is coated with Sin's cum. I will never forget the taste of him.

I close my eyes and let the last tremors of pleasure wash through me.

Alive, I've never felt so fucking alive.

St John

The aftershocks from my release are still rolling up my spine when I let Natalie go, and she slips to the floor. Her breath is ragged, almost sobbing, and I let myself go and slide down next to her.

Her face when she came was glorious. Her eyes rolled back in her head, every muscle in her neck spasmed, her mouth went slack, loose, her lips were smeared with my cum.

I've never had a more powerful release.

I want to lick the tears and blood from her face and then kiss her for hours just to catalogue all the flavours of her turmoil.

Next to me, her breathing slowly returns to normal. She struggles into a sitting position, her forearms resting on her knees, her forehead resting on them. She lets out one long shuddering breath.

"Consent not your thing?" she asks. Her voice is scratchy, but the tone is lighter than I expected.

"It would be inconsistent with my character," I reply honestly.

"If I'd said no, would you have stopped?"

"Yes, and then I would have ripped your tongue out for fucking up my sentencing because actual bodily harm is okay with our bosses!"

"Just as well I wanted it then," Natalie says, and she can't look at me.

"I don't think you know what you want, but it's getting interesting watching you find out."

"What now?" she asks.

With a groan, I push myself upwards, the cut along my ribs hurts; I should probably check it soon. "Now we start cleaning. And you get to do most of the work for being such a shit steward and not doing as you were told."

Cleaning is an essential part of my courtroom ritual, I actually enjoy it, but I don't normally involve my steward. In this instance, I need to keep Natalie occupied while her body chemistry reverts to normal. She risks going into shock if I don't keep her occupied while that happens. She can't be allowed to dwell on this yet.

I'm surprised I consider that.

Cleaning takes over an hour. By the time we are done, we are both sweaty and even dirtier, but the room is spotless, and Cawston's body is bagged, ready to be loaded into the SUV.

When we are done, it's time for a shower. I pull my t-shirt over my head and stuff it into a plastic sack.

It's then that Natalie sees my back.

I know the minute she does because I can feel it. She doesn't gasp or say anything, but I can feel her shock.

I ignore it, same as I always do when people see it.

The state of my back is pretty meaningless to me, it was just another misguided fool trying to control the world, but I know Natalie will dwell on it. Let her. If she ever gets brave enough to ask how I got the scars, I'll consider being nasty enough to tell her.

"It's shower time," I say to her, "Strip."

I find it arousing that Natalie has spent the last hour crawling around in piss and blood cleaning my courtroom, while inside her back combats, her pussy is coated with a slowly drying combination of blood and our juices. It must be sticky and itchy by now.

What a dirty girl my steward is.

I imagine the whole evening has been something of an eye-opener for my little steward.

Maybe she won't come back.

Which would be a shame, because I need to punish her for fucking up my killing so spectacularly.

The throat fuck wasn't a punishment. That was just me getting my rocks off because the pain had made me so hard I couldn't help it. The actual punishment will be much more extensive because clearly she likes it.

I shake my head in disbelief as I open my pants.

"What?" she asks.

"Two years they trained you. Six years they have continuously assessed you. All of that unrelenting psychological pressure and scrutiny, and they didn't fucking notice you're a masochist."

"I'm not."

"Clearly you are," I say as I walk naked to the storeroom and turn on the shower. "You're a slut too, not that that's a bad thing."

She looks mortified.

We leave the body for collection.

I lock the gates of Anathema behind the SUV, and Natalie helps me manhandle it into the metal box by the side of the gate. It will be picked up later. I don't know what they do with it, and frankly, I don't care. It's just cold meat now.

Natalie clambers stiffly into the vehicle. She's tired and worn, but although she is shocked, it's not enough to require any intervention. She must be tougher than I thought. Rose was in shock for a week after our first execution and depressed for months. But then Rose wasn't built for the steward program; she rebuilt herself for it, for me.

My thoughts about Natalie are in flux. I haven't come down yet even though I have had my release - fuck, what a release - by tomorrow, I will be lazy and purring. But right now, my nerve ends continue to jangle and my brain, high on adrenaline, offers up pretty memories for my approval.

I see Natalie's face over Cawston's shoulder, her eyes wide and shocked, her body tense for the blow that was never delivered.

I see Natalie's face as she looked up at me with my cock in her mouth, her lips stretched, her eyes full of tears.

My cock gives an interested twitch.

Natalie pulls her seatbelt on and then curls herself into the corner, as far from me as possible, and my cock hardens further.

I would take round two now.

I could take round two now.

This is the closest I've ever gotten to my deviancy, and it feels amazing.

Cawston's pain, my pain, Natalie's pain, it's like a fantasy come to life.

I hope Natalie decides to stay; there is so much more to explore.

I want to giggle, but that would be truly insane, instead, I smile inside and start the engine.

"Do you need medical attention?" I ask.

"No." Her voice is still wrecked.

"Just checking."

"Just drive. I need to get home and get some sleep," she growls.

Yeah, she'll be back. She's strong enough. She's actually still kinda bossy despite the throat fuck.

"As you command," I say.

She huffs out a barely there laugh, and the tension in the vehicle eases. I pull out of Anathema and turn left towards the highway.

Natalie

Coming home is weird. Stepping into my normal apartment, tidy and boring, after tonight is frankly surreal.

I wearily make my way to the bedroom and strip off, leaving my clothes on the floor before I crawl into bed.

We showered at the carriage house, but I think I still can smell blood.

I went first, scrubbing my body without looking, quickly washing away the evidence of my mistakes and our joint response to them.

When I stepped out of the shower cubicle, St John threw me a towel. By the time I wrestled it around myself, he was under the water. I think he was trying to prevent me from seeing his back again.

I remember his back in the fluorescent light of his courtroom after we cleaned the blood and the piss from its shiny black surfaces. It was in many ways more shocking than anything else I saw in the previous few hours.

He'd stripped off his shirt and the light fell on two curved scars high on his shoulder blades. A hand span wide, they were ragged, twisted, and thick, but weren't the most obvious thing; they just highlighted the real damage.

St John's naked body was beautiful, the skin on his chest lightly tanned and glowing, with a smattering of dark hairs. His abs were smooth, and over his ribs, the rippling gills of his serratus muscles were clean and chiseled. From the front, his body was healthy and whole.

In contrast, the skin on his back is like a lunar landscape under an icy sun. From his shoulders to just above his waist, the skin is bleached and dead looking, tight and white and streaked with rough, shiny stripes.

The muscles moved, but the skin looked reluctant to stretch, pulled tight across the curves of his musculature, the line of his spine a desert valley.

I only saw it for a moment, he knew I'd seen it, but he offered no explanation.

I was left wondering what the hell did that to skin, and how he lived with it. It was clear he still felt the injuries because the muscles jumped and twitched nervously under their skin shroud as he moved.

The phone wakes me so suddenly it feels like I fell off a cliff.

It's not even six am.

"I need you to come in." Rose doesn't bother with salutations, she just belts out her orders.

"I'll be right there," I say, rolling naked out of bed. My throat is sore, and my lips tingle. I shut my eyes and squeeze them tight. When I speak, I manage to control my voice. "Is this about the execution?"

I wouldn't put it past St John to have made a complaint about my actions last night despite what we did afterward. Never trust your instrument was basically the first rule they banged into us.

"Among other things."

"Transparent as ever," I say as I walk into the bathroom and flick on the shower—time for a much more thorough wash. My hair is a rat's nest and I'm sure I have blood in my ears.

I catch a glimpse of myself in the mirror and see the livid bruises Sin left around my throat. I touch them, press my fingers into them, and hiss as sensation ripples through me and my nipples harden.

"What was that, Natalie?" Rose didn't miss much.

"Stubbed my toe," I reply hastily.

"There is the possibility of a new case that matches Sin's skill set."

"Okay, give me an hour," I reply, "Just got to shower and eat something,"

"You can eat? I didn't eat for three days after my first execution."

My mouth floods with saliva. I'd forgotten, too caught up in what had happened afterward. The images rush in and overwhelm me. The red ruin of Cawston's throat, the look on St John's face as he saws back and forth, maximizing the pain, the way he presses his knee between Cawston's shoulders and nearly cuts his head off.

I drop the phone and vomit into the toilet, my stomach churning as a cold sweat bursts through my goosebumped skin.

"That's better," Rose says, her voice tinny over the phone's speaker. "I was getting a bit worried there for a moment. You sounded too normal. Make it two hours, and I'll see you in the office, Natalie."

"Thanks a fucking bunch," I speak to the bleep of the disconnect tone and close my eyes.

Bad idea. I'm assaulted by sensory memories, the smell of the blood, the sound of Cawston's last gulping breaths.

I retch again, bringing up only bile.

"Good, you're here." In her usual hunch over her desk, Rose makes notes on a printout, her crabbed hand scribbling on the page.

I take a seat and cross my legs, glad to be back in business attire instead of combats and casual shirts. It makes me feel more normal. I'm even wearing makeup and I put my hair up.

I sit quietly, waiting for her to give me her full attention. The coffee I mainlined sits uncomfortably in my empty stomach, but I needed the caffeine kick when all I wanted to do was crawl back into bed and forget the world for a little longer.

"How did it go?" Rose doesn't look up from her work, violently scoring out line after line.

"Okay. I haven't got my report done yet, we didn't finish until late. I'll have it for you by the end of the day."

She lays down her pen and finally looks up at me, peering over her glasses. "Did St John need any sort of release afterward?"

"That's a delicate way of putting it!"

A corner of her red-lipped mouth twitches and her eyes are assessing. "Please don't hedge around me, Natalie."

"Yes, and no."

She leans back in the chair. "Tell me."

I drop my head, unable to meet her eyes.

"Oh, I see. You were the release."

I nod dumbly, and heat climbs my cheeks.

"What happened? Did you fuck?"

"Oral," I mutter. I still can't look at her. I don't know if I am ashamed, horrified, or just ruined. I'm thinking probably ruined.

"Okay."

I risk a glance up at her. She looks nonplussed and turns to her computer screen and starts clicking away.

"That's all you have to say? Okay?"

She glances at me. "Well, it's not ideal, it's a little quick, but it's not exactly surprising either. We'll just have to see how it affects you working together over time."

"So instruments fucking stewards is okay in your book?"

"We don't actually have a policy about it. It's not normally an issue we need to consider."

I'm not sure if I'm relieved or furious. Part of me is very serious about my responsibility, being a steward is a huge deal, and having sex in the courtroom feels like a violation of the role. On the other hand, I don't want my career to be over because of this.

Rose turns away from her screen. "You seem confused."

I shrug. "Look, the last few days have been something of a mind fuck, and last night was the mother of them all. I'm just really confused about how St John and I having–" I search for a euphemism, "–contact, the way we did, fits into the whole instrument–steward dynamic. It just seems–" I struggle again for the word, "–wrong."

Rose leans back and her eyes are shadowed. She pauses, gathering her thoughts. "Last night was your first time stewarding, and I am sure, as is the way of it, that your expectations of what happens in a courtroom went right out the window."

I nodded.

"There are textbook scenarios, and then there is real life. It's like surgery; textbooks are full of neat, clean drawings of anatomy, but the inside of a human is a gory mess that looks like someone put a butchery counter through a blender. That's what happened last night; you graduated from studying anatomy to watching surgery."

"I'm pretty sure blowing the surgeon is frowned upon."

She gives me a quick on and off again smile. "If it was what he needed would it be? The circumstances are different, but the comparison is the same. Real-life is messier than the theory, infinitely so when we deal with fraught and frightening situations. Nobody is sure how it will pan out in the field.

"I'm not saying you did well, and I'm not saying you did badly. I haven't seen your report yet. You both walked out alive, and a killer is no more. At this point, I am more interested in establishing you and St John as a viable team, and it looks like sex or sexual attraction are going to figure into how that works."

I shake my head again. "I don't think we covered ourselves in glory as a team."

"Well, you don't look too battered, so you're already doing better than anyone else who ever tried to work with Sin, other than me. So I would say you're not off to the worst of starts."

"You seem pretty invested in me staying in the role."

"St John is used to people being scared of him. They are mainly scared of him because, you know, they meet him when he is about to kill them. Or they are paid to be something he will get off on, and that doesn't make for lasting relationships. Or they are new stewards shitting themselves over his reputation. His only long-term relationship has been me, and ours is not the kind of relationship that can evolve or even last much longer, whereas your relationship might."

"You brought me in to fuck St John?"

"No, I brought you in to replace me. You and he decided to make it sexual."

"I wouldn't say I decided."

"Did he rape you?" Rose sits up in her seat and her eyes go flat with anger. I guess I found where she draws the line.

"No, god, no."

She relaxes. "So it was consensual."

"It wasn't non-consensual."

"Stop hedging, Natalie. Did he do anything you didn't want?"

"No." I am sure of that.

"How do you feel about it now?" Rose again takes pity on me, her voice is softer.

This morning I was sick to my stomach at what I had seen, but not about what I had done with Sin.

I vomited because, well, because I'm human. Despite me knowing that it was justified and sanctioned, my body responded illogically, viscerally, to witnessing a violent death. But once the vomiting was out of the way, I felt okay. I actually feel okay, not revolted, terrified, or guilty. I feel okay, as if vomiting was part of the processing.

I guess Rose can see the thoughts on my face because she leans forward and rests her chin on her fists. It's an incongruous position for an old lady, but it's natural, her focus is on me. It feels validating.

"I went through the same process you are going through, and I used to ask myself how I could do it, how I could be mentally okay with it?

"But I could because I was trained that way, and I have a psychological bent that allowed that training to stick. You are the same; all the best Stewards are the same.

I shake my head. "But I messed up, and then we..." I make a helpless gesture.

"We all mess up to a greater or lesser degree. This is not a clean, clinical process, if it was, it wouldn't be the kind of deterrent it is. This is a messy, violent, unspeakable process, and that is why there is only one steward, and a certain flexibility is permissible."

I nod.

"But that does not mean there is no oversight." She leans back in her chair again. "Never forget that. I expect your report to be filed by midnight tonight, and we will discuss it at your first supervision. I expect it to be one hundred percent truthful.

"The version that reaches the permanent record will be redacted of whatever you and St John did afterward, but the version I see will be the whole truth. Do you have any questions?"

"Just one," I say, and then I look her straight in the eye. "Did you pick me to be his girlfriend?"

She laughs. "No, Natalie, I picked you to be his steward. What happens after that is entirely up to you and St John.

"I will say this though, you have the potential to actually have a relationship with him, no other potential steward had that. There were some that could have worked with him, with coaching, and that would have been fine, but someone who could relate to him? Well, I thought he deserved that."

Her expression tells me I can't expect anything more in that line of questioning.

She reaches for a file on her desk. "And now on to other things. Let's talk about this new case I have for you and St John."

I'm surprised. "You still want to give it to us?"

"Yes," she says evenly, "because you need to get back on the horse after you fall off, and this time you are in at the start, and that's important.

"You have to learn to work together, not just kill and fuck! And remember, just because we go to dark places, it doesn't mean we have to stay there.

"Now pay attention, because this case is interesting. Consider it my peace offering to Sin for landing him with you."

I lean forward in my seat as Rose outlines the case.

Chapter Six

Natalie

I go home and change before I head to St John's house. I take off the business pantsuit and throw on leggings and a hoodie. I leave the make-up on, for some reason I want to look like a put together woman but not a formal one. I feel this is going to be a tricky moment in our relationship.

It almost feels like the first date after first sex and that's a really stupid way of thinking about it.

The pretty row house is quiet when I let myself in, no music, no sound of keyboard or TV. I find it hard to call out to St John, to let him know I am here, but I don't want to just wander around his house looking for him.

I can smell coffee, so I toe off my shoes and head into the kitchen. St John never said to take shoes off in the house but it feels polite.

The kitchen, like the other rooms I have seen so far, is spotless and white. The accent colours here are a little darker, more a French grey than a pale grey, with stainless steel appliances.

There is a mug of coffee on the pure white marble countertop and a Post-it note is stuck to it - *Patio* - It has an arrow underneath pointing towards a wide arch that leads out of the kitchen into the living room.

I sling my messenger bag across my body and pick up the coffee. It's still hot, and fragrant with nutty notes. I take a sip, it's creamy and a little sweet, comforting on this chilly October morning.

The living room is calm and charming. A wide fireplace has a fire already laid in it. The mantle above holds a trio of plain stone figures, chunky and ancient-looking, rough approximations of people in light, textured granite. On either side of the fireplace are built-in shelves. St

John must file his books by colour. Clearly only ones with white spines or pale blue covers are allowed in here.

Why does that make me smile?

I cross a thick white tufted rug that breaks up the continuing expanse of golden floorboards and step into a small conservatory that runs along the back of the house.

Sin is naked in the privacy of the courtyard garden. He moves through a series of yoga poses and my mouth goes dry at the sight of him.

He has no right to be as beautiful as he is - his height, the long lithe lines of his muscles, and more than that, the way he moves them, uses them, controls them. He is all about the control - over his body, over himself, over his prey, and now over me. He knows I am looking at him and he chose that, the time and the place to be naked before me.

The morning sun is gentle on his skin, touching him lightly as he finally comes to rest cross legged on a yoga mat. His eyes open and he looks at me, amber fire in the depths of them, his face expressionless because he has no need to offer me an attempt at human.

Slowly he rises from his cross legged pose, and I try to keep my expression as blank as his. I don't think I manage it.

His body has a thin sheen of sweat on it despite the chill of the morning. His uncut cock hangs from a well-trimmed thatch of dark hair at his groin. It's a gorgeous cock. I had it in my mouth when it was thick and hard, the veins pumped and the head exposed by his arousal. Now, seeing it soft I still want to take it in my mouth. I want to nurse on it and the thought shocks me more than what we did last night.

Sin doesn't rush to cover himself. The way he accepts himself makes him even more beautiful, like he knows just what he is, and he's happy with it, and that enhances all he is. It's not arrogance, it's ease.

He moves over towards a sarong folded on the wrought iron chair and wraps it around his narrow waist. He makes the simple cloth look intensely masculine and I mourn the loss of his naked self.

All the times he hides his true self is for our benefit, not his. Shielding himself from our gaze is an act of kindness, one of the few he is capable of.

He likes being himself, and that is a powerful thing. I have heard people label the Instruments many things, but he isn't a fallen angel, he's not a forgotten god, he's not even a monster. He does what we ask of him, pure and simple and deadly. He knows exactly what he is worth, and it is respect and fear.

I respect him, I fear him, but I feel something more as well, and I shouldn't think that way.

Sin looks at me as he ties his sarong, watching me thinking about him. He raises an eyebrow, questioning.

I shrug, wordless, and he seems to understand that.

I find myself sinking down to sit on the step from the orderly living room to the sunny courtyard. He moves over and sits beside me and we both look out at the perfectly ordered, narrow, limestone paved, backyard. It is a riot of autumn colour.

"Hey," I say quietly. He turns and looks at me, his face more relaxed than I've seen it before. He is sleepy-eyed, his thick dark hair tousled. He looks replete and relaxed. "Shouldn't you cover up, you don't want to catch a chill?"

"I run hot," he says, and I can feel that's true as his body heat bleeds through my top and my leggings from how closely we are pressed together in the doorway.

I take a sip of coffee and feel myself settle inside as we sit quietly and enjoy the sunny morning. It is calming, watching the occasional spiral fall of a flame red leaf from the cherry tree, the slow waft of the grey grasses in the side border, and the burnt orange flowers of the shrubbery that forms a backdrop to the seating area and firepit at the far end.

The yard is surprisingly private. The high fence and the trees of the neighbours gardens make it feel sheltered and intimate.

"Thank you for the coffee," I say softly.

"We're not friends, Natalie."

"Come on, you like me a little bit. I'm not that bad?" I press my shoulder against his. I can sense his moods now, and his comment wasn't delivered with his usual acid.

"You have a good mouth," he says huffily, and takes my coffee from my hand, sipping it himself.

"Do we have to talk about that?" I've done nothing but think about it since it happened, my mind replaying it in perfect Technicolor widescreen, with added special effects.

"Don't ruin my state of mind." His long toes flex restlessly on the brick of the step.

"Okay, going to shelve that for now then."

We sit in silence for a moment. I wonder what sort of a person this makes me, that I can sit in companionable silence with a killer who damn near choked me on his cock last night after having garrotted a man in front of me.

I guess I'm an example of what the training can do.

"We have a new case," I say, and he turns and looks at me curiously.

"Really?"

"I know, it's fast. I thought we would have more shakedown time, but Rose called me in early this morning. I have the details in my bag."

He raises an eyebrow. "Have you looked at it?"

"Glanced."

His eyes narrow, and it's like I can see his brain turning. The satisfied predator that was relaxed and licking his bloody claws turns his head to see another meal step into the sunlight and finds it is still hungry.

He rises in one sinuous movement. "Well then, time to get back to being an utter bastard."

I feel the relaxed mood slipping away.

"Take it into the office I'll join you shortly."

"Is it more sex workers?" he asks when he joins me in the office. He is dressed in olive green combats and a cream Henley, the long sleeves pushed up to his forearms. His hair is damp and tousled from the shower. I catch the scent of bergamot as he passes me.

"No, I don't think so, not specifically anyway. Why?"

"I like avenging sex workers, and it happens a lot."

I didn't know that, that his cases were often sex workers.

"They say there are dangerous jobs, cop, fireman, saturation diver, but its sex work that is the most dangerous, and the least likely to be solved because nobody gives a shit. Old stereotypes die hard. I rather like changing that. I rather like choosing to deal with these cases, and not just because the people who kill sex workers invariably go on to kill those outside the demographic - they're not big on asking for ID. It's because justice is supposed to be blind, and I see everything."

I wonder if it is because of his past. I know there is trauma there but nobody knows what it is. I wonder if where he came from and who he was influenced how he sees his role. Did his family throw him out to become some forgotten statistic, missed by the system, falling through the cracks, brutalised in secret because nobody cared enough about him? Is that what drives him?

We're advised not to think too closely about what made our instruments the way they are, it's a pointless question, but I have a special connection to psychopaths, I want to know where they come from, and so I can't help thinking.

"So you have a personal reason for choosing to get justice for sex workers?"

"Well I avail myself of their services."

"That wasn't what I meant."

"I know, but that's the truth. I like them. I like the honesty of their work. And those I have procured have always been satisfactory, unlike other professions."

Why am I jealous? Rose told me he uses sex workers, she gave me a list of vetting ones when he asks for one. Did I think now he had me he wouldn't need them - that's a fucked up thought.

"I think everyone should take a stint as a sex worker," he says casually, "It's character building. It also helps them gain skills in the bedroom."

I feel like he is baiting me. Inside I am shivering, I want to ask the ridiculous question - Was I good enough.

I would rather bite my tongue off than ask it.

He laughs as he leaves the room.

I hate that he knows what I am thinking, that I am transparent to him.

"Let's see what Rose has sent, and then we can discuss your appalling performance yesterday and what we're going to do about it."

There must be something very very wrong with me because I'm frightened of this man. Even when he is seemingly relaxed, I know what he is, and yet, I like it.

I like him.

And when he shows his claws, I like him even more.

"Hey, I thought you said I had a good mouth? And now you say my performance was appalling!"

"That was the only thing you did right last night."

He settles into his office chair and crosses one long leg over the other. I see his thigh muscles flex and I remember the lean power in them as he flexed through positions this morning.

"Like I said, we're not friends," he says looking up at me, "and you are not up to my standards yet, not by a long way. The new case is clearly a peace offering from Rose for having to put up with your sorry ass."

I feel like mouthing off but I haven't got a leg to stand on here, I did fuck up last night, professionally, and I need to accept that I have a lot to learn.

It is ridiculous how fast Sin's moods, Sin's house, this strange back and forth between us is becoming not just acceptable but my new normal.

I should be traumatised. I should be doing everything possible to get the fuck out of this situation. I'm not.

I woke up horrified. It passed. I woke up knowing what we did was sick. It doesn't seem to matter when I see him and feel his strange, enticing charisma.

Maybe we all secretly yearn for that sensation of shivering fear with someone who is truly dangerous, and yet we trust.

Why do I trust St John?

Because I don't disagree with a single thing he's done so far.

St John

I keep the execution work separate from my translations. I have a large table and a whiteboard in my office that is specifically for casework.

I like to lay out all the evidence so I can look over it at any point. I'm not keen on computer imagery, I like to touch the real thing, which is why Natalie has a whole file that she takes from her messenger bag and starts to arrange on the table.

I press up against her side, jostling her, trying to see what I've been given this time. This is always an enticing time for me, getting ready to dive into another deviant mind, hopeful of challenge and fascinated by comparison, similarities, and differences.

"Stop it," Natalie growls and bats my hand away when I reach for a crime scene photo. "Let me lay this out and then we can go over it."

I pout and step back.

I sulkily finish my coffee.

"Right, showtime." Natalie steps to the side so I can see the table. "We have three killings - three seems to be the magic number this year - and the only similarity I can see is victimology and a pretty small area."

I chew my lip and quickly scan the layout. Fair play to her; Natalie has laid this out logically. I nod in approval.

"All the killings took place close to the university within the last six months. The victims were, once again, down and outs, vagrants, two men, one woman."

Natalie points to the first section of the table. "The first killing was Abi Taylor, fifty-five-years old, no fixed abode, been on the streets for decades. She was battered to death outside the university library, her usual place to bed down. She was well known amongst the student population and wasn't known to be troublesome, just kind of shouty, but harmless."

The beating the women succumbed to was intense. She had been battered around the head, her face was a mass of contusions. I could see where the bones had shattered under the skin. A chaotic, rage-filled kill.

"Cause of death was skull fracture," says Natalie.

I nod and pick up the close-up view of the crime scene. The body is a bundle of rags up against the grey, graffiti-marred wall of the library building.

I put the photograph back on the table.

"Okay?" Natalie asks, and I nod. "Victim two was two months later, strangled."

I pick up the second photo. "He wasn't just strangled."

"True. According to the autopsy, it was more like he hanged."

I examine the photo. An elderly man is slumped in the doorway of the university observatory. I pick up another angle of the scene and nod slowly. "This is rather nasty. His hands and ankles were broken, and a ligature looped around his neck and attached to the door. His bodyweight killed him because he could neither lever himself up nor use his hands to free himself despite being low to the ground. Interesting."

Natalie sighs. "If you say so. His name was Brian Albany, mid-fifties, again long-term homeless, and a bit of a fire and brimstone preacher. He was known to wander around the parks offering to pray with people."

I raise my eyebrows; this is becoming more and more interesting. I peer closely at the photo, and something tickles in my brain. I just need my subconscious to stop being shy and give up what it has noticed.

I gently place the photo back on the table. "And the third victim?"

"Now we get into very weird territory," says Natalie. "This victim was found naked, tied to a tree in the parkland beside the university. He died of hypothermia."

The photo she hands me shows a paunchy, wrinkled older man, the tattoos across his torso so old they are mainly blue smudges. Bound to a young tree, his head has fallen to the side. He looks quite peaceful.

"I'm not entirely sure why this case has passed to us," Natalie says, "I'm not sure this is a serial killer."

"Oh, it's definitely a serial killer. An evolving one at that."

"What makes you say that?"

I sit down on the sofa and rest my elbows on my knees. "The first kill is chaotic and violent, a sudden outburst. Something triggered our killer, and he just exploded.

"The second kill is sadistic and nasty. I think that was our killer realising that the first kill met some need within him. The third kill was more organized but no less angry. Also, the third kill is humiliating."

Natalie looks inquiringly at me.

"An elderly man, likely a former sailor by his tattoos," Natalie checks the victim profile and nods, "is tied naked to a tree and allowed to freeze to death. That feels humiliating to me; that feels like taunting the victim with his own nakedness and powerlessness.

"So we have sudden anger evolving into sadism refining into humiliation. This feels like mirroring."

"You think the killer is punishing surrogates for events in his own life?"

"Maybe." Something else prickles at me. There is no point trying to force it. I need to let my brain offer up its ideas.

I stand and go over to the table. Leaning down, I peer at the photographs again. The tickle in my brain isn't interested in the victim photos, it's sending me back to the scene photos.

"We have two victims on university grounds and one victim on adjacent land?" I confirm with Natalie.

"Yes. The medical examiner puts time of death for all of them as late evening of the day before they were found. Apart from the library, which appears to have people around it at all hours of the day and night, the areas were very quiet. The observatory is particularly known for being a quiet place on campus."

"I think it would be an idea to visit the crime scenes as soon as possible," I say, "Something is pushing me towards the scenes as a connection rather than the locality. Although the victimology is interesting too."

Natalie's stomach growls loudly, and she rolls her eyes at me. "Sorry, not eaten since yesterday."

"Come on; I'll feed you," I say.

Natalie follows me into the kitchen and hops onto a countertop while I pull sandwich fixings out of the fridge.

"Off!" I snap. Her eyes narrow, but she slips off the marble, taking a seat at the counter like a civilized human.

She moans greedily and wolfs down the sandwiches I make her. Watching her pink tongue dart out to lick mustard from the corner of her mouth and then swipe a dribble of mayonnaise off her thumb reminds me that I need to punish my little steward.

She has been a good girl today, bringing me an interesting case, but she was bad yesterday, and I want to remind her of that.

When she gets up to take her plate to the sink, I lazily reach out and grab her wrist. She tenses and turns to me, her eyebrows raised in inquiry.

"You haven't forgotten we need to arrange your punishment, have you?"

She swallows and her pupils go wide.

"Maybe punishing you will help me get the case straight in my head. "You're very keen on teamwork, aren't you, Natalie? Fancy taking one for the team?"

I rise from my seat and lean in close to her; it's fascinating that she cannot take her eyes off my mouth.

"You can't punish me," she whispers, trying for bravado.

I push her back against the fridge, my thick hand over her throat, reclaiming the bruises I put there last night. I slide my thumb up and down where her carotid artery lies buried in the muscle of her neck. She knows I know how to shut it down. Her eyes are glazed, I want to make her needy for me.

"I can punish you, and I will if I want to. We both know you'd like it. I see the slut in you, Natalie. You can't hide it from me now I've seen it in all its glory."

I can feel her pulse hammering against my thumb, and she can't rip her eyes from mine. I press a little harder into her neck.

I lean forward, let my lips ghost along her cheek before I whisper in her ear. "But today, I'm relaxed. I'll keep your punishment for when I really need to let off steam.

"Maybe today I should just have you warm my cock while I think my deviant thoughts, or work through the crime scene photos looking for that one all-important detail..."

My brain fires, gives up the answer.

I release Natalie's neck and step back, leaving her to slump against the fridge.

Now I realize what was prickling at my brain, what connects the cases. There is an additional element, a ritualistic element, hidden in plain sight in a really annoying way.

I should have spotted it straight away.

Natalie is more of a distraction than I thought.

I turn and hurry to my office.

Natalie

He leaves me floundering, again. One second his hand is on my throat, my every breath is his to control, and the images his growling voice paints are right there in front of my eyes. The next second he is gone.

I am wet, horny, confused, and bereft, all at the same time.

Taking a deep breath, I pull myself together and once again trail after him into the office wing, like a moth to his flame. It's an unfortunate analogy because I realise more with every hour that Sin could burn me badly.

St John is leaning over the case table. He smiles, slow like honey sliding from a spoon. "Gotcha," he says quietly.

"What?" I step towards him.

My heart is still pounding as I move close enough to see what he sees. He glances at me and smirks as he notices my hard nipples poking through my shirt. "Look." He taps a photo. "That is if you are not completely distracted by how wet your pussy is right now."

I nearly stick my tongue out at him.

The frantic flip-flopping of emotions that have characterized this day is catching up with me fast. Any second now I'll start stamping my foot.

Actually, thinking about it, it feels like this day started at least forty-eight hours ago.

Between capture and execution, sex, my body's revolt, followed by confession and investigation, all on three hours sleep, both my body and my brain have been through the wringer.

"What?" I say.

"Fucking Enochian!"

"I have no idea what you are talking about?"

"There is a connection other than victimology between these killings, and the connection is Enochian."

"Yeah, still drawing a blank." I knuckle my eyes and wish for a soft bed, preferably full of Sin and I. My lips wrapped around his cock, suckling it while I fall asleep - I was never submissive. What the hell is happening to me?

"These markings here, and here, and here." Sin stabs at the three crime scene photos. He lifts the library photo and shows me, his finger on the wall behind the victim. "Those markings are not graffiti, they are Enochian, a language dreamed up by a sixteenth-century charlatan and purloined by a twentieth-century cult leader."

I lean in and look closer. There is a meaningless row of symbols among the colourful layers of tags and scratched names on the library wall.

St John picks up the second photo. On the observatory, the same symbols are scratched into the white plaster running parallel with the ground.

The symbols appear again, around the edges of a ragged love heart cut into the tree's trunk where the third victim died.

"Did the analyst who transferred the case to us mention this?" St John asks. He turns away from the table and sits down at his computer.

"I didn't see anything in the notes."

"If he was experienced, he may have noticed it subliminally and that was what set him to tie the cases together." He taps rapidly at his keyboard and then writes down a series of symbols on a post-it note.

Rising, he snags a magnifying glass and pores over the photos again, glancing at the post-it for comparison.

"Yeah, Enochian, it's the word *HOATH,* which translates as *The True Worshipper.*"

The strange word sounds like he is gargling gravel.

"You can read that shit?"

"No, I can tell you what those symbols are meant to represent; the term reading isn't quite accurate."

"You're going to have to bring me up to speed here, Sin. I can see the evidence, but I really don't understand what it means." I pick up the post-it and look at the strange symbols.

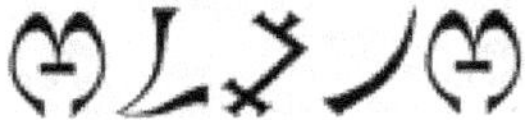

"Is this one of your ancient languages?" I ask.

"No, it's an invented language, more like a cipher." St John returns to his seat and waves me to the sofa. I sink into it gratefully.

"In the sixteenth century, a polymath by the name of John Dee got fooled into thinking he could communicate with angels."

"As you do!"

"Well, yes, as you did back then. He was actually a genius, way ahead of his time mathematically and scientifically. If this angel shit hadn't sidetracked him, he would have been as famous as Galileo. Unfortunately, back then, the sciences were a much broader field and included alchemy and scrying.

"Dee was led to believe, by a scryer called Edward Kelley, that he could communicate with angels who would teach him the language that God used to create the world.

"Kelley gave Dee a series of letter codes which purported to be the angelic alphabet. A year or so later, Kelley provided a series of poems, or chants, which he thought would give him the keys to enlightenment."

St John scratches at his chin, which is dark with stubble. "It is a fascinating story, not least because it is the tale of a great mind led astray by wishful thinking."

"Clearly this is important," I say, "But what's the link between this and our killings?"

"Well, Enochian, or Adam's language as Dee was fond of calling it, was pretty much forgotten until in the early twentieth-century interest in it was resurrected by one Aleister Crowley."

"Him I've heard of."

"Yeah, Crowley has found his way into all sorts of modern stories, but he was another brilliant misguided man, no doubt with serious demons of his own, led astray by impossible quests. Although in Crowley's case, the quests were mainly about enticing multiple partners into bed with him.

"He resurrected Dee's works on Enochian and wrote about it, calling it a powerful system of magic. Ever since, people who claim to be his followers have been messing around with it in various forms."

"How come you know about it?"

"I love ancient languages. I study them, and I had a look at Enochian twenty odd years ago to see if there was any possibility it was a real language."

"Is it?"

"No, it's totally made up. If it was as ancient as it is purported to be, it would behave in a different way. Written languages evolve the way they do due to necessity, Enochian doesn't display that evolution. Essentially, its English syntax with weird symbols."

"But you knew what that series of symbols meant, you even spoke them."

Sin grins. "Impressive aren't I!"

"Dick."

"Thank you."

"It sounded like you were crunching rocks."

"Yes, in its verbal form it's quite rough on the throat." He smirks again and side-eyes me. I smother my own smile, it's not as rough on the throat as he is.

He grows serious again. "That particular sequence of symbols forms a well-known word; that's why I recognized it. It has an established translation and is in one of the 'supposed' Enochian keys given to Dee. Being able to pronounce it isn't that impressive in my field; it's similar to being able to say abracadabra and know the origin."

St John looks as though he is about to launch into another lecture so I hold my hand up. Fascinating as his knowledge is, and alluring as I find his way of expressing himself, there is more at stake here.

"The use of the symbols clearly is a new link between the killings. Do you think these are ritual killings?"

St John looks wary, as well he might; ritual killings are not in his wheelhouse. He's supposed to be kept away from them.

"I don't think they are necessarily ritualistic; there isn't any associated paraphernalia. But the use of the symbols narrows the suspect pool significantly. There may be a link to Crowley's fan base. Unfortunately, his brand of *do as thou would* hedonism has spread far and wide."

"Time for research then," I say, "I need to get up to speed on this if you think it is important."

St John looks thoughtful. "I know it is important, but I'm not sure in what way. That word is accurately reproduced, but something about it doesn't feel right; it doesn't feel magical, for want of a better word. I need to think about it."

I can see his gaze turning inward.

"What can I do to help other than get some background on Enochian?"

"I would say run a search for any advocates of Crowley and his particular brand of magic locally, but it's so popular now you'll be inundated. You can also get me more background on the victims."

"Okay." I get up and stretch, noting that Sin allows his eyes to drift over my form. I stretch a little further, arching my back, allowing my shirt to tighten across my chest. "What are you going to do?" I ask.

"I'll do the same, make inquiries my way, and we'll meet tomorrow to examine the crime scenes." He smiles suddenly, a dark and dangerous smirk. "This is so much more interesting than the last case."

"Only because you're not supposed to be doing it."

He flicks a glance at me under his eyelashes, "You might be right, little steward," he says, "I rarely get to be naughty like this."

"Why do they keep you away from ritual stuff?" I ask thoughtlessly, and the gates slam shut. His face goes cold, and I suddenly remember I am in the pen with the tiger.

"Because they are stupid," he says with contempt, "they think ritual was something important in my past. That it's triggering for me. They're wrong, but I am bored of telling them."

"The fact that you can read an ancient ritual language probably doesn't do your case a whole heap of good," I say, because clearly I have a death wish.

"Just because I can understand it doesn't mean I believe it," says St John acidly, "In actual fact, I believe it less than they could possibly imagine. Thinking I can speak to god is never going to be a trigger for me."

"So the whole Enochian thing means nothing to you?"

"Not spiritually, no," he replies. "It just means I know what playground we are in."

"I should really send it back, though, shouldn't I?"

Sin looks at me with narrow eyes. "No, it's mine now." he sounds almost greedy.

"Are you sure? If this is ritualistic, and you're not supposed to do ritualistic, then we could be on sticky legal ground."

"Time for you to fuck off now, Natalie, particularly if you are going to report this." His eyes are cold. I don't like it.

Silently I pack up my notes and push them into my messenger bag.

"I'm not going to report anything," I say quietly. "We're a team now, right? I'm on your side."

"If you say so, Natalie." He doesn't even turn and look at me. He's on his computer, pulling information into his den for consideration.

I quietly let myself out of the row house and go home.

I am on his side. I saw a spark in his eyes when he recognized the Enochian. I saw the sharp interest, the fire in his mind. I want to work with him on this, watch his intellect stretch to beat this puzzle.

And at the same time, I'll be working on the puzzle that is St John.

Chapter Seven

St John

After Natalie is gone, my space seems less alive, less vibrant. I think I miss her. Explaining things to her triggered new lines of inquiry in my head, like she's a catalyst for my brain. It was never like that with Rose.

And she is much nicer to look at.

I know I baited her and teased her with punishment, but is it wise to bring more sex into our workplace?

Maybe I should have told her she could stay longer, bed down in Rose's old room tonight if we worked late, it's why it's there after all.

The idea of her being under my roof is strangely appealing.

I've never had a pet, maybe Natalie can be my first - most people start with a goldfish.

It is important to train pets.

I like the idea of training Natalie.

My mind returns to Natalie's body. I saw it clearly last night, not in the courtroom where my focus was just on the pleasure but later, both before and after she showered. It is quite lovely, and I am drawn to her – her soft skin, smelling of summer flowers, her ripe breasts, her beautiful muscles and her greedy mouth. She is enticing in ways I've never experienced before.

Sexual attraction doesn't usually linger with me. It is done and dusted, and the person never mattered because people are things, but Natalie, there is something different about Natalie. I want to make her scream, kiss it better to taste the difference, then hurt her again just to make sure of the flavour.

I imagine taking her when I want, where I want, because she is mine.

I've never wanted to own someone before, it causes a strange sensation in my chest, like a tightness.

Even Rose, I can take or leave. If I never spoke to her again, I would be surprised because she is a part of my life, but I don't know if I could 'miss' her.

Natalie though, she has been gone barely half an hour and I already want her back.

I made such a beautiful mess of her last night. I'd like to do that again.

I dim the lights in the room, it's nearly dark already, the quick winter afternoon already over.

I let my mind drift. Leaning back in my chair, I adjust my cock in my jeans. After a release like last night's, I am normally uninterested in sex for longer than this, yet I'm half hard just from the memory. My brain is helpfully conjuring scenarios where I can pry even more secrets about Natalie's sexuality out of her.

She was so desperate when she was messy with blood, her lips stained with it, and I fed my cock into her mouth, and I wonder what she would look like if I fucked her. How would she take it?

I want to investigate her pussy, then wreck it. I want to make it swollen and wet, make her so turned on that I can slide my finger in alongside my cock when I fuck her. I want to stretch her so open she hisses and her hips stutter as pain mixes with pleasure.

I want to work her so open, make her so fucking needy that she will take whatever I decide to press inside her and take it willingly, with loose limbs and hooded eyes.

I want to bend her in half and grind myself deep inside her, deeper than anyone ever went before, while her hands on my thighs claw and grasp because she wants more, more, more.

I free my cock from my pants and stroke it lazily. In the shadows, it's easy to imagine my Natalie obeying me. I like her fighting back like a scratchy little kitten, but I like her more when she obeys.

I spit on my hand and stroke myself harder, twisting my wrist at the head, working my foreskin over my glans, squeezing pre-come from my slit.

Fucking Natalie would take time, deserves time. Right now, I would just make a mess of her, make her needy for more. I imagine telling her to strip for me, down to her panties, and then making her bend over the desk in front of me. The view would be delicious, her lithe thighs spread wide, a lacy red thong clinging to her high round buttocks. I would slide my chair closer, pull her thong halfway down, just below the crease of her ass, to trap her, then I would examine her. See just how pretty the holes between her legs are, how much I need to stretch them to take me.

Natalie doesn't strike me as an experienced player, so it will be fun to introduce her to the pain, desire, and intense emotions that rough pussy pounding and deep anal evokes.

I wouldn't finger her or lick her out, well maybe one lick, just to taste her, get a flavour of her juices, but I would want to run my hands all over her, finding her sensitive places.

She will have to earn my cock inside her. Part of her punishment will be being denied it until I'm ready to hurt her with it.

Relaxing further back in my chair I close my eyes and make the pictures of Natalie clearer. My grip on my cock is firm now, my strokes fast and long, and I use my other hand to roll my balls, tugging them lightly.

I imagine rising and blanketing Natalie's body with my own. The thick material of my combats would feel rough against the back of her legs, my t-shirt warm against her back. I would hold her down with my weight and press my cock into the space between her thighs, trapping it against her warm, wet pussy, rutting the blunt arrow of my cock head against the sensitive spot where her clit hides.

I'd want her to know she doesn't deserve me inside yet.

I'd whisper, "Close your thighs," and she would, giving me a delicious warm channel to fuck.

"I am going to make such a mess of you, little steward." My words would cause her to shiver and push back against me, straining for friction against her clit, friction I would deny her because this would be just for me.

My orgasm is close, I can feel it rising. I don't bother holding it back, jerking myself fast and rough, just letting the tide of it rush through me. I imagine my cock growing fatter and harder, rubbing relentlessly against Natalie. As I bring myself off, I imagine coming across her pussy lips, spurt after spurt flowing over her plump lips and dripping down her thighs while I drag my spasming cock through the mess.

I sigh with pleasure and roll my head back against the soft leather of my chair. Thoughtfully, I lick my fingers clean. I spend the afterglow imagining pulling Natalie's thong back up and then making her clean my spent cock with her sweet mouth, while her pussy throbs with denied arousal and her panties are stained with my cooling cum.

It is full dark and cold when I decide to leave the house to speak to the street people. I can't settle despite my orgasm, so I might as well start my investigations among the victims.

I dress down in old combats, broken-in boots, and a parka with a beanie pulled low over my hair.

Outside, the air is icy with the promise of first frost. I hunch my shoulders as I make my way towards the soup kitchen that operates a few blocks from the university's south entrance. I should find some people there who knew the victims, and even if I don't, I can slip them a few dollars for their time.

Out here, in the night, this is the closest that I get to normal. I'm just another anonymous, invisible person, indistinguishable from all the others who fell through the cracks.

I drift around the edges of the clusters of people gathered around the well-lit soup kitchen run out of an old food truck in an underground car park. I stick to the dark edges and listen before asking questions.

All these people had a chance at different lives, just like me, and they didn't get to live them for one reason or another. These are my brothers and sisters, unlucky, fated, damaged, addicted. I am all of those things and more. I guess that's why I feel calmer out here with them.

It makes me angry to think people see them as prey, substitutes for their real enemies, decoys to take out their deviance on, as if they haven't had enough shit thrown at them.

I can't change their lives, but I can at least punish those who treated them as less than human.

Before we assume the mantle of Instruments, they give us an option to end it. And it's fucking tempting, let me tell you. I really thought about going to sleep and not waking up. Not having to be me, just being gone. To be honest, I've never been entirely sure why I didn't take the suicide option, but when I'm down here among the homeless and the dispossessed, I get an inkling of why. I think it's because there is still, maybe, hope of a better life. If I don't get it, at least I make sure others don't get their chances taken from them.

Maybe somewhere deep inside, I believe in redemption, that for all the wrong I so clearly am, I can be better.

Whatever the reason, I refused the suicide option although the majority take it, the percentages are something like sixty/forty, or maybe they are fifty/fifty now, but whatever the statistics, many like me choose to go to the eternal black rather than wait for it to find them.

Fucking psychos, control freaks all of us.

"Hey brother, can you spare a smoke?" I turn at a familiar voice making a regular inquiry.

"Sure." I take a packet of smokes from my pocket and hand them over. "Take them; I was giving up anyway."

Mustard is nearly blind, but he can still pick me out in a crowd. "I thought it was you," he says, and pockets the smokes, knowing there is more than Marlboro in any pack I give him.

"They don't call you Mustard for nothing."

"Keen as mustard, that's me, never miss a thing." His chuckle is low and cracked. "Anything I can help you with? I got a feeling you's looking for info."

"Always," I say. "Want to go get something to eat?"

"Can I bring my dog?"

"Of course." I know a diner not far away that will let Mustard's scrappy little terrier in so long as we sit at the back and the dog stays under the table.

"Looks like Christmas is coming early," Mustard says happily.

"Do you need a hand?" I offer to guide him.

"Na, it's good man, I can follow you through this mess easy enough. You smell a lot nicer. You're like a flower in a shit field. Even with my fucked up eyes I know where you are."

"I always wondered how you could find me in a crowd."

"Now ya know."

He shuffles along with me as we make our way the two blocks to the side street diner. The place is empty apart from us, one waitress and the short-order cook flirt with each other just for the practice.

I order at the counter and guide Mustard to the back of the diner. He shuffles into his seat, and his dog scuttles between his feet.

Mustard gobbles up a monstrous plate of burger and fries and noisily drinks three cups of coffee. "Man, this is the life," he groans and pats his belly when he is done. "Time to pay the piper now then." He looks at me hazily through his cataracts. "What do you need to know?"

"I'm interested in an old woman who used to sleep up by the library, name of Abi Taylor. She met an unfortunate end recently."

"Abi The Bag," Mustard nods. "Yeah, I knew her. I heard she was gone but I don't know nothing about it."

"I'm just interested in her. What kind of person was she?"

He scratches the scruff on his chin with a thick yellow thumbnail. "She was okay, harmless, mad as a box of frogs, though. She thought the world was ending any day now, but she wouldn't hurt a fly, might yell at one, but never hurt it."

"I heard she'd been around a long time."

"Yeah, she's been on the streets as long as I have, years and years, always tried to get a place to sleep at the library, she had a sweet spot there, under an overhang."

The library is a remarkably ugly building. Built in the early 1970s, it hasn't stood the test of time well and needs renovating. It is as if someone tried to take the grace of classical architecture and recreate it by carving out a block of elderly cheese with a blunt knife. It is slabby and unwelcoming, with a brutalist edifice that looks derelict, like the kind of place fire teams practice rescues.

However, due to its excessively blocky architecture, it provides overhangs and shelves where the homeless in the know can find shelter and a quiet place after dark to sleep.

It sounds as though Abi was one of them, having her own claimed corner.

"Did she go there every night?" I ask Mustard.

"Pretty much. She always said she hated the place though, thought it was a terrible waste. She told anyone who would listen that books got no use, might as well burn them to keep warm."

I grunt, libraries are my long-time love. While I might hate the building, any home to books deserved to be cherished.

I ask Mustard about the second victim, the old brimstone preacher at the observatory, but he doesn't know him or the sailor in the woods. He tends to stick to his patch of well-lit streets and busy areas and avoids going into the quiet areas.

"Thanks for your time," I say eventually. It's clear he has no more information to offer me, but at least I have more of a sense of Abi now, so that is something.

Casually I slide some notes across the table to him. "How about you and the mutt find somewhere warm for the next few nights. The forecast is cold; you should have a roof."

He peers myopically at the notes and they vanish into one of his many pockets. "I might take your advice on that. It gets harder every year."

"You don't need to leave when I do," I say. "Stay here until they close. I'll tell the waitress to keep you coffee'd up."

"Thanks, man, I appreciate it."

"No problem." I rise and begin to pull my parka on.

"Hey, man," Mustard says, "If more of the street people are dying, you make sure you deal with it for us, okay?"

"I will," I say seriously. Like I said, he's well-named. He might be blind as a bat, but he's keen as mustard.

Natalie

It is early evening when I let myself into my apartment. I don't know where this day went. Hell, I'm not sure where the week has gone. I'm tired but wired. I won't be able to sleep yet, and I don't actually want to go to bed and then wake up staring at the ceiling at two a.m.

Instead of crashing, I change and go down to the pool in the basement. Swimming is my exercise of choice and it always helps me calm down. The steady cut through the water, the stroke, stroke, breathe into the channel of air that runs alongside me, the touch, the turn, it's like meditation, a ritual that clears my mind.

There is ritual, and then there is ritual.

When we talk about rituals in our line of work, we literally mean rituals, with candles and skulls and chanting - and cases involving rituals are rare.

We're not talking about the TV show psycho-babble about killers having rituals that are not connected to the way they kill - you know, taking a lock of hair, arranging the body, masturbating on a cactus three miles southeast of the dump site, etc. Those rituals don't really exist, or our people have never found them to be particularly prevalent, certainly not enough to be useful.

No, we're talking about actual fucking ritual, esoteric sigils, weird-ass herbs and bones, the mystic stuff. That is a category all of its own.

It turns up in all forms of voodoo kills, and it's nearly always there with the seriously deranged. In our experience, when brains go haywire, they take the baseline influences in their lives and extrapolate them out-wards.

So it's pretty natural that in a country where religion is a big deal - either embracing it or denying it - we're going to get our fair share of killers who are inspired, driven, or seduced by quasi-religious source material.

As a nation, we may grow out of it. Chances are, thirty or forty years from now, we'll have a killer who we will endow with nicknames like. "The Instagramer" or the "Facebook Flayer," ritually killing for likes, hearts, or thumbs-ups. But right now, religion remains the driver, inspiration, and trigger for a lot of the weirder cases.

St John is supposed to be kept away from those cases. St John, according to his profile, doesn't need that sort of case on his roster.

And I find myself wondering if Rose has an inkling that this case has a ritualistic element. Maybe it's a test. I decide to keep that in mind moving forward, even though doing so makes me feel paranoid.

I shower by the pool and then return to my apartment, make myself a cup of tea, yet another ritual, and sit down in front of the computer.

I'm a good girl, I'm going to do my homework.

I start by opening up biographies of Crowley and John Dee, tabs on Enochian language, theories and uses, and Washington Satanist groups – yes, that's a thing.

My chair isn't as comfortable as St John's, and I wriggle on it.

My apartment is just a base and it shows. It's close to the department, close to amenities, and not too far from bars if I need a hookup (rarely, no time). It lacks the charm and character of St John's place.

I keep promising myself I'll make it nicer, but I never seem to get around to it. India doesn't care on her rare visits. If I fancy a warm body, I go to their place or book a hotel.

It's a nice place and spacious because I'm not hurting for money even though I'm not in the same league as St John. I've got two bedrooms and two baths, it's a good neighbourhood, and the building has a gym as well as the pool.

Still, St John's house feels so much more comfortable.

God, this Enochian stuff is tedious, and utter horseshit.

I read up on Aleister Crowley, who seems to be both more and less than St John's dismissal of him. I decide not to mention to St John that Crowley also came from a wealthy background, was well known for his unnerving stare, and one of the quotes he is most famous for, "*Certain actions produce certain results,*" could essentially define St John's life and work.

Yeah, best not mention that. I am wary of the punishment I've been threatened with because St John doesn't make idle threats. The punishment will happen.

On the occult side of things, I find Crowley dismissed in public but studied in private, which leads me to think our killer may be less a wannabe satanist and more of a serious student. I make a note to mention this to St John and consider drawing up a psychological profile of the kind of person who would be academically interested in Crowley's work.

I'm trawling through online forums of wannabe Satanists with increasing irritation when I randomly open another tab and go looking for info about a family that lived on an estate on the Potomac and called one child per generation St John and pronounced it like the English do. Hey, I've read an occasional classic!

I find St John's family with one short keyword string and a couple of clicks. Research is my bitch.

The house and land where Sin has his courtroom was owned until twenty years ago by the Morton Miller family, wealthy farmers and community leaders, who had farmed the banks of the Potomac River since the 1720s. According to the historical building registry, it's now owned by an unnamed trust.

There is no information about the current St John Morton Miller. Of the previous generation, there is little other than a funeral notice from twenty years ago.

There is copious information about the many previous generations, including historic home records and a really awesome collection of photographs in various archives.

I bookmark them for further study if I feel so inclined.

Then I return to the glaring hole in the records and consider it - my St John (funny how my brain works), according to my reckoning, is St John Morton Miller IX. I could go and try to ferret out his past, but that feels wrong.

I tap a little tattoo on the keyboard; I'm kinda itching to know, see what I can dig up and try putting two and two together to see if I can find out what made St John.

All knowledge is power.

But Sin is the first person I have met in many years who just fascinates me for himself.

I never expected that.

I figured I would do a bare minimum stint as a steward, retire out of it and go into policy. Until now, all my interactions have been based on keeping me on that track. Now, the first instrument I ever spend any time with is so frightening, so fascinating, that I want to really know him. Him the person, not him the killer.

Researching him any more than I already have feels like cheating. Not only that, it feels unsatisfying.

Sin is the book you don't skip to the last page to see if your guesses are right. Sin is the book you read slowly and savour.

Yeah, I'll take my time. I'll go through those old photos at some point because they are genuinely fascinating, particularly as I now know the place and have a connection with it. But as for trying to work out Sin's story from whatever traces of it are buried online? Nah, I'm not going to do that. I want to hear it from his lips.

I close my eyes and remember his lips. How firm they were, how his kisses were brutal, but his tongue was soft, and his skin, under the metallic tang of blood, smelled of black pepper and lemon, invigorating and fresh.

My phone ringing jerks me guiltily from my reverie.

I scrabble for it; it's St John.

"Hey," I answer, clumsily closing browser windows as if he can see me over the phone.

"Just checking in, letting you know I've been out, and now I'm back."

"Is that a thing?"

"Well, you get my trace records so I thought I would tell you to save you wondering where I went."

All instruments are chipped. Getting sent their trace records is another part of the steward role. I can't imagine needing to go through them in anything other than an emergency though.

"Uh, I wasn't planning to." I get the impression that calling like this is out of character for St John.

"That's decent of you. I find I can tolerate you, little steward. Everyone else I've ever worked with was on my death list within forty-eight hours. Despite your lack of discipline last night, I wanted you to know that you're doing okay."

"I've heard of your temper," I say. He nearly beat one steward to death, and another has a permanent limp because of him. Two others immediately retired from the service after time with him.

"Yeah, you don't want to see it. What time did we agree for tomorrow?"

"We didn't."

"Shall we say nine a.m. at my place? I can make breakfast."

"You are offering to make me breakfast? What happened to the evil killer I have grown so quickly attached to?"

"He's out buying poison for the pancakes."

"I'll see you tomorrow." I know he can hear the grin in my voice. "Goodnight."

It amazes me that I have already lasted longer than anyone else, every other steward placed with St John, other than Rose, was gone by now or in need of serious therapy.

I'd feel proud if it wasn't for the sneaking suspicion that my lack of serious damage is because I was okay with him sticking his cock down my throat. I'm so okay with it that I'd like him to do it again.

He woke something in me, something that wasn't planned and organised, thought out and backed up. He woke the part of me that understood my sister, that understood him, that had seen death and not been repelled by it. Turns out I had my own monster inside too, and it was just starting to sharpen its claws.

(There are things you plan for, and things you fight for, circumstances dictate what they will be.)

Women, down in their lizard brains, are drawn to the stronger, the more dangerous, mate. Some of the most deep seated triggers to arousal are seated in that paradox. I know that, I've read the books.

But to the best of my knowledge there has to be an element of comfort, an element of trust to accompany those feelings of being together with the dangerous and the strong. And Sin doesn't give me that. He gives me the reverse. So my lizard brain should be freaking the fuck out, and sometimes it does, but never for long enough to make me quit.

If that wasn't so fucked up it would be interesting.

Chapter Eight

Natalie

I am quickly coming to the conclusion that Sin likes to show off. When I arrive at the row house I am again directed to the patio. Unfortunately he is not totally naked this time. Instead he wears a loose pair of yoga pants and his chest is bare.

He has a long narrow blade in his hand and it is as though he dances with a shadow opponent.

It is one of the most beautiful things I have ever seen.

Sin spins and twirls, his balance perfect, his feet firm on the ground. His hands never stop moving. They conduct a symphony of death in the air in front of him, both the hand carrying the blade and the empty one.

In some ways the movements seem formal, in other's they are totally random. I find myself becoming mesmerised by them, trying to discern the pattern and rhythm. There isn't one, it's just grace and power and a contained evil.

The knife looks wicked sharp.

Finally he stops. He is panting slightly and her muscles are flushed with blood flow, pumped up with the veins in his forearms crawling across his skin.

We stare at each other.

"Wouldn't a gun be more efficient?" I ask.

"I don't like guns, they are boring," he replies, and slides the knife into a thin scabbard he picks up.

"That's a weird looking knife."

"It's a stiletto."

"Like the shoe."

"Yes, like the shoe."

I feel a lecture incoming.

"It was developed in the middle ages to penetrate chain mail."

"Handy in twenty first century DC."

"Handy in any close quarters." He's brisk this morning, maybe I should have made my appreciation of his form more obvious. "It's an assassin's knife, and the style I was practicing was Paranza Corta, Italian knife fighting developed to utilise the stiletto blade. Sometimes it's called Schema Di Siciliano and I find it relaxing to use."

Of course he does.

"Why all the hand waving? Although that is very Italian."

"It's to stop the enemy being able to focus on the knife, it's very disorientating to face."

"I'll take your word for it."

"I hope you do, I'd hate for you to find out the hard way."

"Is it going to be one of those days where I get threatened a lot?"

He seems to consider that.

"No," he says begrudgingly, "We have too much to do today."

I pick up the cashmere sweater he has left folded on the arm of the sofa just inside the conservatory. I hand it to him. "It was amazing to watch," I say, "Like dancing with death."

He huffs but I can tell he is mollified that I noticed. Every male has an ego, even the psychopathic ones.

St John's pancakes are a work of wonder, and my stomach feels pleasantly full after them. I'm a happy little steward when we set out to walk to the crime scenes. Sin only lives half an hour's walk from the university, and as it's a fine day, we decide to hoof it, heading to the observatory first.

It's easy to forget that we're about to visit a location where someone suffered and died when Sin is so charming and easy. Off his home ground and far from his courtroom, he seems approachable and human, smiling at me as we walk side by side towards the observatory's famous formal gardens and reflecting pools.

"I knew this place was here; I've just never been," I say as the white dome of the observatory comes into sight above the brightly colored trees.

"It's a beautiful building," Sin says, "with nothing in common with the library."

He told me over breakfast about the information he'd gathered about Abi, the library victim. I've spent a lot of time within the library's brutal architectural embrace. I think I actually saw Abi herself once or twice, as I left after a late study session. When Sin mentioned her being known for saying she would burn the books to keep warm it triggered a memory. I recall an old lady with a shuffling walk muttering about setting the library on fire to keep warm.

We follow a brick path through the formal gardens, and the observatory's elegant frontage comes into view. Its classical facade is beautifully balanced, tall and square with high windows and a porticoed entrance. The building shines brightly in the morning sun, seeming almost otherworldly with its domed eye to the sky.

"Is it open? Can we go inside?"

"Someone is excited by this field trip!"

"Don't be a dick." I mock glare at Sin's smirk. "I'm a guy, okay? I like telescopes and stars and shit like this."

"No argument from me," says Sin, "But no, we can't go inside. Visits are by appointment only, and the observatory itself closed a long time ago, once Washington started making it impossible to see because of the light pollution."

"Shame." I make a note to bring India here. She would love the gardens and the building even if we can't go inside; it's obviously a quiet space, which is good for him. I don't think we've seen another person since we entered the gardens.

Sin walks up to the main entrance of the observatory, but I hang back. I'm more interested in getting an overall view; he can scrutinise the symbols up close without me.

I drag my eyes away from the way his black jeans stretch over his ass as he squats and examines the remainder of the building.

A small brass square is set in the second story above the entrance. I fish my phone out of my pocket and run a quick search. It's a sundial from Ireland, made by the priest who founded the observatory.

"Hey, Sin." He looks up at my call. "You know this place was founded by a priest, right?"

"Yes, I do my homework."

Asshole, I think affectionately, and wander over towards him, still eyeballing the scratched symbols. "And it's positioned exactly north-south, the guy who built it determined the exact longitude and latitude of the city."

"Yes, I know all that." St John is still squatting by the door, his gaze intent on the Enochian.

"Do you think there is a connection between that and the killings?"

St John slowly straightens up, his thighs flexing. "I want to say, no. I want to say fuck off, that's all a bit Da Vinci code, but there is an obvious connection and I can't ignore that, much as it annoys me."

I look at him inquiringly.

He huffs out an annoyed breath. "It's like someone is playing with lives and symbols and what they think they see. That always pisses me off. Killing isn't clever, and it generally comes down to sex or power. Making it try to mean something else is just a form of lying."

I stay silent.

"I've seen a lot of nutters, Natalie," he says wearily, "and I've seen a lot of killing. No matter how the deranged mind tries to disguise it, the motive is always sex or power and generally both when you get to the root of it. I try to look past the symbolism; it's generally a superficial reason."

I nod, that makes sense.

"The people like to make the world a more complex place than it is, crime is not always that complicated."

"It seems complicated to me."

"That's your brain buying into the stories."

I look at him questioningly.

He sighs, "Everything is stories, baby, the stories we tell ourselves, the stories we expect."

I file away the "baby" for later consideration.

"It's like all the nightmare scenarios that people believe but which never happen. Everyone believes in red rooms on the internet. Places where people are tortured and raped on the instruction of faceless third parties watching and paying for their sick thrills in bitcoin. The red rooms don't exist. The dark web isn't what people think it is. The internet did not make people bad, it didn't even make them worse, it's just another bogey man amongst a host of others. Families are the worst, they always have been. What people do to those they are linked to by blood is always going to be the most common hell."

"What about you," I say, "Surely you are another bogeyman, another type of story, and you're real."

"Yes," he says, "I exist, and I'm allowed to, and I'm probably one of the worst things humans have come up with. What I am saying is that the people think the dark web is deep and the deeper you go the worse it gets, that's not true. The real depravity is hidden in plain sight. And it's me and all the others like me."

"You think you are one of the worst things humanity has come up with?"

"What I do is one of the worst things, releasing people like me onto the streets to kill those who don't obey your rules."

"You don't agree with the death penalty!"

"Of course not, it's barbaric."

I stare at him.

He smirks at me, "And so am I."

Compassion for him nibbles at me. It suggests, somewhat stupidly I feel, that I should offer him a touch, a human way to communicate that I don't think about him that way.

He is just as likely to break my fingers as accept any uninvited touch from me.

He watches me consider how to react as a human being to his words. He quickly grows bored.

"Come on," he says, "let's take a look at the woods. I've got what I need to from this scene."

We leave the university grounds behind and cross a road to the wooden gated entrance to the park. It's a semi-natural area, a haven for wildlife, and runs the length of a stream-cut valley. Sin says he jogs here often in the summer because the trails are shaded.

We walk in silence for a while, our boots silent on the damp dirt of the leaf-strewn trail.

"You say you've seen a lot of nutters," I venture. "Does your back story include one?"

"You're determined to get this story, aren't you?"

I shrug. "I think it's important."

"Not really, and you could just go and look it up. I'm sure you have enough information on me to find it now."

"I didn't want to; I wanted to hear it from you."

He glances at me. "Well, that's at least respectful." His smile glimmers through and I respond to it. Here, under the trees, he seems less wild animal, more human.

"I was briefly famous once, but you wouldn't have heard about it. It happened before you were born."

I know St John is in his mid thirties, and I'm twenty-eight, so whatever happened, it must have been when he was very young.

He puts his hands in his pockets and moves like a normal man, nonchalant, relaxed, at ease in the fall sunshine; it almost feels like a first date, if it wasn't for what he is about to tell me, about the making of a monster.

"I was the Lindbergh baby of my time. Only not so little, and not so dead.

"I was taken at six years old. I was found at eight and a half. My family abandoned me when I was eleven because they couldn't cope with what I was. That's the timeline."

Our steps slow, and I want to watch his face when he tells me this, but this must be hard, even for Sin, and I don't want to make it harder.

"The man who took me believed I was an angel and did everything in his power to make me reveal myself." Sin's voice is even, not shut down or fighting emotion, but settled, as if this is something he accepts as naturally as breathing.

"At first, he sat for hours in front of me chanting. As time went on, he yelled names at me, trying to make me respond to my *true name*.

"He tried a lot of ways to make me show angelic self. Eventually, he tortured people in front of me so I would save them – which shows his stupidity because the way to save them would be to kill him. His logic was that crazy.

"If I had been an angel, he would be dead. But he didn't seem to care, he just wanted to see the angel. If he had a plan for after that he never shared it."

Sin shakes his head. I can see him biting his lip. It's not fear or pain that makes him do that; it feels like frustration.

Sin keeps his head down, and we keep slowly walking.

"I saw people flayed and disembowelled before I was eight years old, and it was done just for me. I used to think I could see the ecstasy in their eyes at the end, just like the martyrs in the old paintings. I assume that was my brain grasping at straws."

I don't know what to say. I want to reach out and touch him, offer some form of comfort to the child he'd been. He obviously feels my emotion; he is probably used to the reaction. It must have happened a lot.

"Don't feel sorry for me." He looks at me, a rueful expression on his face. "In all honesty, I was wrong even before he got me."

"You think you were born wrong?"

"I was born different. He didn't make me what I am."

I nod; I can understand that. I raised India as far as I could, as long as I could; her brain is different from mine. I know that for a fact. She isn't evil, evil is an overused word, but she's not neurotypical, and neither is St John.

"My backstory is why they keep me away from ritual killings," he says, "They think it means more than it does."

We step off the path and move through the thicker growth to where the crime scene is marked by the limp hanging remains of police tape.

"Dicks," says Sin. "I hate that they leave this stuff lying around." He gathers up the remnants of the high vis tape and rolls it into a ball, stuffing it in his jacket pocket. That's my instrument, the tree hugger, annoyed by tape when a naked man froze to death here, the thin skin of his back rubbed raw by the abrading bark of the tree as he tried to struggle free.

Again, I stay back and let Sin assess the evidence close up.

I can't see any symbolism here.

The ground around the tree is well churned, but that's likely from the police officers and forensic teams.

The tree itself isn't particularly striking. I know trees have magical significance, but this isn't a rowan or an oak or anything intrinsically special. It's just a random tree.

Sin's nose is right up against the tree as he examines the symbols carved into it.

He nods to himself and steps back.

"Anything?" I ask.

"Yes."

"Going to share?"

"Not yet."

"Way to go, team!"

"Come here."

I step forward, and Sin puts his hands on me. I immediately respond, my body tensing, my pulse rate rising.

"Easy, little steward." His eyes glimmer in the sunlight through the trees. "I just want to position you."

He presses me against the tree then steps back.

I stay in position, and Sin's eyes on me are slow and stripping.

He prowls around me, the human gone, the animal is at the forefront, assessing the scene.

I feel tension vibrating in the air. Sin adjusts his cock in his jeans and my body responds to him. My libido watches him constantly, looking for signs of desire, yearning for them. I try to push down the surge of heat in between my legs. This is wildly inappropriate.

What does Sin see? Does he see me, or does he see an old sagging sailor, frozen cold and hard by rigor, stiff in his bonds?

It doesn't matter really, his eyes are on me, and I like that. I fight it, but I like it.

"Okay," Sin steps close again, "I've seen what I need to see." His voice is gentler again, his eyes normal; the beast is back behind bars.

"Helpful?" My voice is hoarse again. Sin has a ridiculous effect on me.

"Very, thank you." He smirks at me. "I'm building the story in my head. Seeing you there helped."

"Glad to be of service."

"Are you, Natalie?" He steps closer and runs a thumb over my lower lip. The fucking monster. "Because this scene was all about humiliation. Do you like humiliation?"

What can I say? If Sin is dishing it out, then probably I do.

When I think about what Sin told me about his background, his trauma, I wonder at what point during his ordeal he went mad. The things he went through, surely only madness comes out of enduring that as a child?

He says he was always wrong, that he was born this way. All the kidnapping did was give his deviancy a path to trot along. He never did the whole discover you're a monster thing that many others do - animal torture, abuse of others, manipulation, all the evolving.

Sin says he stepped out of captivity a fully-fledged killer. He didn't need to evolve; he knew what he was.

Our brains forge pathways, little electric connections, and I can see how Sin's brain got to be wired the way it is. It doesn't mean it has to stay that way; brains can be rewired.

You see, I'm not a *glass half full* or *glass half empty* kind of girl. I'm a *the glass is refillable* kind of girl.

Sin's family had connections and money; they made the problem of the damaged little victim go away. But did they jump to conclusions? Is Sin truly a psychopath? Does he deserve the label he wears and the job he does?

In some ways, it clearly suites him, but that doesn't mean he should live his life within a gladiator circus. I think of Akrotiri, of the ruins and the frescoes, and I think he deserves to see them.

They built the early onset program for Sin, because of Sin. The instrument system for serial killers was in its infancy, and Sin's family looked into his cold yellow eyes and thought, that's convenient, and threw him in there. They threw him away.

St John is a killer, St John is a deviant, St John is damaged, but is he still trying to be what other people tell him he is?

One man thought he was an angel.

His own family thought he was some kind of cursed thing.

What if he is neither?

He says he doesn't have a heart, but what if he does? What if he just hasn't heard it beat yet over the sound of the screams?

Or am I just kidding myself because I have a case of lust exponential for a man who states he could kill me without blinking an eye.

St John

"Let's skip the library today," I say to Natalie as we leave the park. "I found out about it last night, and I want to go home and think now."

She nods in agreement, and we head back to the row house. I wonder what Natalie thinks of my story.

She got the bloody bare bones of it and that's normally enough to stop most people asking more. It's a weird and horrible tale, something people don't mind reading in books, but hearing it from the source tends to be too much for most people.

Apparently not for Natalie.

"How did you get rescued?" she asks as we walk down the hill towards my house.

"I didn't get rescued," I say shortly. "The police didn't find me. The private investigators my family hired didn't find me. One day he just let me go."

I remember that day, how the sunlight hurt my eyes, how the outside air smelled dusty and excessive, and how the sky was too big above me, like a big blue bowl filled with screaming emptiness.

Natalie fishes the key I gave her out of her jeans and opens the front door for us. That's a noteworthy thing. She does it so casually as if she belongs here already.

We make our way into the kitchen, and I rummage in the drawer by the coffee machine for something caffeine-rich and dark. I feel like a rich roast after examining two crime scenes.

"What happened then?" Natalie clearly wants the whole story.

I sigh and open the coffee machine, sliding in a pod. "He put me in a car, drove out to the highway, and told me to get out." The coffee machine whirrs and spurts hot water. I hold up another pod for Natalie, and she nods absently, her eyes fixed on me.

"I don't know why he let me go at that point, but he seemed confident, as if he had had an epiphany." I roll my eyes at the religious reference. "He had taken to calling me cherub, and he said he'd be back when I finally grew my wings.

"I sat down on the side of the highway, which turned out to be in Utah. I remember it was hot. A while later, a police car pulled up; someone had reported a shirtless boy sitting on the side of the highway."

I hand Natalie the first coffee and start my own.

"They took me to the station, and I remember the greedy look on their faces when they realised who I was. They thought they were going to be famous, but they weren't, because my family kept my return very quiet.

"They were never sure what they were going to get back. Turns out that was wise because they got me."

I glance at my phone to check the time. I have an online meeting shortly, but I have time to finish this part of my story.

"Things didn't get better when you were found," Natalie guesses.

"No, they didn't," I say wearily. "Hospital, police, parents, doctors, therapists, therapy, and interviews, it was all a blur for a while. I didn't like it any more than I liked being shut in a room with my captor. In fact, I liked it less.

"It took my parents just over two years to throw in the towel, not that they made any grand efforts in that time.

"And then Rose came along, and things got a bit easier for a while."

"She took care of you?"

"She was my foster carer and my tutor in the Early Onset Program Dr Goodlove was developing."

I finish my coffee. "Much as this bonding exercise is apparently useful for you, I have something else to get on with."

"Oh." Natalie appears nonplussed.

"I do have another job," I remind her. "My days can't be all fun and frolics in the woods imagining you naked."

She grins at that, all sexy plush lip smile and sparkling eyes. Shame it doesn't really work on me.

"I think I'll drop by the library, take a look before I go home and get back into the research."

"I don't want you investigating on your own," I tell her. "You haven't got enough mileage on you yet, and I would rather be there with you."

"Pah," she scoffs at me, "you go out on your own."

"I'm a trained killer. I'm the nastiest thing anyone could encounter. You aren't, and you could spock our killer clodhopping around being all official."

She purses her lips - that's the thing with the steward-instrument relationship, nobody is quite sure who is in charge. I mean, obviously it's me, but Natalie may well believe it is her because she's not a serial killer.

I lean into her space and breathe on her neck, watching my warm breath send a shiver through her. "Remember the punishment, little steward, it's still coming, and if you mess up my nice new case, I will make it much worse than I planned."

"Research it is then," she says quietly.

"Good little steward." There's that shiver again, God she is adorable. I want to blow off my meeting and play with her all afternoon.

There is little doubt in my mind now that my work with Natalie will retain a sexual component, her responses are just too enticing to ignore, and it's obviously not going to drive her away. In fact, it seems to be lubricating our working together. Maybe there is nothing like a little workplace flirtation to increase productivity. I'm amazed I got to find that out!

Chapter Nine

Natalie

"Hey, Monster, how are you doing?" I haven't spoken to my little sister in a few days, but she doesn't seem to mind.

India glares at me. "Growing up so I can kick your stupid steward ass," she says, and then giggles.

It's going to be a good day, and I smile at her.

Maybe it isn't a great idea to nickname your sister after the worst thing she could become, but it's the elephant in the room; ignoring and tiptoeing around it would make it worse. So she's my Monster, and we own it together.

That's the thing I try to make India understand, no matter what, even if she prefers it, she is not alone. She is loved. I hope that makes the difference for her, because Sin never had that, and after spending time with him, I believe more than ever that it could be the missing piece.

Sin would sneer at me but fuck him, he doesn't know everything, and I'm going to keep on trying this.

"Can you come out today?" I ask her.

"Nah, I fucked up this week. I'm only allowed out into the park for half an hour." She doesn't appear bothered, but little bothers her other than rules she thinks are stupid.

I don't ask what she did. It's not really important.

"Wanna go see the stick with one end?"

"If you tell me what your Stewarding was like."

"Not a chance," I say breezily.

"You're no fun."

"Like your deviant little mind needs more fodder in it!"

"True," she admits without rancour. That's the program, accept what you are, learn to leverage it, own and control it for the greater good.

I don't need to give her a blow by blow (no pun intended) of my abysmal first performance as a steward, she's only interested in the death throes anyway, and it's not ideal for me to place myself within her imagery.

"How about we go throw a ball around instead?"

"Yes, it will be good for my co-ordination. Growing this fast is fucking with my reflexes at the moment."

I shake my head at her. "Yeah, because that's the go-to reason for playing."

"It is the evolutionary reason for playing."

"Shut up, smart ass, and get a coat."

She discretely flips me the bird and goes to get a jacket. I make eye contact with her tutor and she just smiles.

"She's good today, go play," she says. "She was antsy because she knew you were Stewarding this week, but she's okay now."

I don't hide stuff from India. I might not be willing to give her the details, but she needs to live in this world, so I told her when I was assigned an instrument. She probably understands it better than me how much risk that involves.

She may be only a kid on the outside, but on the inside, she is a mess of impulses and desires, just like St John, and she understands the dark drivers more than I ever will.

It's hard to believe when we throw a baseball in the park and she trash talks me, running and jumping, playing like a normal, gangly, growing into her height kid. That is until I trash talk her back, and the next ball is aimed straight at my head. Only my reflexes save me from a painful blow.

I glare at her. "That was a nasty move, Monster."

She shrugs. "You deserved it."

"Fucking didn't," I reply and pocket the baseball. "Come here."

"Don't want to."

"Fucking come here, India," I grab her arm and manhandle her to the bench by the pretzel sculpture.

"I was just keeping you on your toes," she whines as I plop her down on the seat. I don't know how much longer I'll be able to do this without using sneaky tricks. She's getting bigger, and she has been training in close combat since she got here.

"Why do you think I need to be kept on my toes?"

"Because you're in the field now, with an instrument." She looks at me sideways. "You're with St John."

"How do you know that?"

"We whisper in the night."

It breaks my heart to think of them, the instrument candidates, in their 'studies' whispering through the walls, finding ways to communicate with the other little monsters. The program keeps them apart as much as possible, giving them controlled interactions with normal people so they get some social skills, but they are always going to want to communicate with others like themselves.

"So the Monster grapevine spread the word." I hand her the baseball to give her something to do with her hands.

"Yeah," she picks at the stitching on the ball, "what's he like?"

I sigh, "Not so funny as you," I push my shoulder against her, "but he's okay, we're going to be a team, we're going to learn to work together, that's the plan."

"Is he scary?"

"He can be," I admit, "but he's really good at hiding it too. He walks around, talks to people, and he's got a really nice house."

I don't want India to become an instrument. I want her in a nice clean lab taking out her issues on viruses and pathogens. But if she does end up going the instrument route, she needs to know she can still have a life, circumscribed and bloody for sure, but with more freedom than she has now.

"Are you worried about me?" I ask carefully. It's hard for India to put a name to a feeling. We try to avoid doing that because she gets upset about her lack of them, even though she does seem to have some residual emotion for me as a sister. I am different from the other humans that are around her; she barely notices them. There is still an attachment between us, albeit a chaotic one on her part.

India is carefully considering the question, digging deep inside herself to try and identify an emotion and label it.

"I think so," she says eventually. "It's like I don't really see other people, but I see you, you're like a weight in my world." God, I love her deviant, strange, beautiful mind. "And it's like as long as you are there, I have something to go around, something to orbit, not like you're my sun, but you're like my..." She gets frustrated, and her picking at the stitches becomes more frantic, I gently reach over and take the ball from her hand before she rips a nail off. She growls at me, squint-eyed and suddenly furious.

"Take a breath," I say, "try again, consider the definition of the words, keep going until it sounds right in your head."

Obediently, she breaths, she knows this works with us.

"Orbit is wrong, but weight is right." Her breathing slows, and I can see her digging deep into the mess of impulses, desires, and confusion that is her mind. Suddenly her eyes light up. "Lodestone! You're my lodestone; you show me the right way."

I feel a burst of joy. What a thing to be to my little psychopath sister. I grab her and hug her and ruffle her hair. She squeals and bats at my hands. I laugh, tell her she is awesome, and that I will stay safe for her.

She is gasping for breath between giggles when I pull back. "St John isn't a threat," I tell her. "St John will keep me safe. He's going to be my team, like I'm yours."

"Okay, but if he isn't, when I finish growing, I'll take him out."

"Fair enough," I say, who can argue with that. She's still a Monster, but she's my Monster, and I have no problem loving her.

Maybe that's why I'm drawn to Sin. He and India are similar. There is the same darkness in Sin but also the same light, it's a weird light for sure, like a storm light, but it's still light.

Sin is edgier when I arrive at his place the next morning. I decide it's not worth beating around the bush with him, same as with India.

I ask him what the fuck is up and he responds to that.

"It was strange to recount my story to you."

We're in the kitchen, and while the day is dark and gloomy with rain dripping down the windows, the space is still bright and inviting.

"I realise that it is a long time since I have told my story. Everyone else who needed to know heard it long ago."

"It was useful to hear it," I tell him. "It's what new colleagues do. It helps us get to know each other, to work as a team."

"Wasn't fucking your throat enough?"

"Dark, Sin, very dark," I say sternly.

"I've had a dark life," he looks around the sunny kitchen. "Not that you'd tell from this. I guess it's why I like it bright and light in here."

"I did wonder." His house is the epitome of a comfortable, light-flooded space.

"It's a nice house," he admits, "I liked it from the start." He sounds almost wistful. "But I do still spend time at the house on the Potomac. I do wish that had turned out better."

He burned his family home to the ground as soon as he came into ownership of it.

"Have you ever considered living in the carriage house?"

"No, it's a killing space."

"How does that work when you stay there then?"

"I sleep in the garden, in the summertime."

That's no weirder than many of the things Sin does.

"Why did you choose the carriage house as your courtroom. You could have had something built for you anywhere you liked. I've seen courtrooms in warehouses, basements, I even saw one in a garden shed."

"Ahh the infamous *tours of the killing fields* section of the steward course."

I nod. "Yeah, your place is never included?"

"They only use old places, defunct places. I'm still in operation. Frankly, I'd rather have a stranger look at my colon than my killing room." His humour is sly and dry.

"Do you know any other instruments?" I ask, remembering India's comments from the day before. Do they still whisper to each other when they are grown?

"No, we're not encouraged to form connections among each other for obvious reasons. I know the statistics, and I hear a few names now and then," Sin says. "I did bump into Annabel one night when we both happened to be following leads in the same place - I suppose that could happen more often than it does."

"Annabel is dead," I say, without thinking.

"Oh, I didn't know that."

"Sorry, it was a scenario that came up in training, that's the only reason I know."

"Don't apologise. I don't care."

We drift back towards the office; we seem to gravitate between here and the kitchen.

"Her steward was rather careless of her," Sin says, "and she seemed flightier than me in the few moments I spoke to her."

She had been, she'd been fucking deranged, a really bad fit for the instrument program, which is why she is dead and so is her steward. I don't expand on it with Sin.

"Do you stewards connect much?"

"Don't know, I've only been in the field for a week, haven't had my invitation to the monthly hoedown yet."

"There's a monthly hoedown?"

I laugh. "You are so clueless about some things, of course there isn't." I grin at him obnoxiously. He narrows his eyes, and I tense, that's been logged for future punishment. I shiver inside.

"They train you guys on your own, don't they?" I'm thinking about India again, denied company and contact.

"Yes, we really don't play well with others, and we have to be trained to fake 'relationships.'" He makes the adorable finger quotes that I find charming and stupid at the same time - here's St John, the curse of careless Stewards, being silly.

"They teach you how to have relationships?"

"No, they teach us not to kill everyone we come into contact with."

"Fuck off, that's just the mythology; you're no more a random raging killer than I am."

He grins, a sudden wide grin that gives me hope. "True, but I like messing with you too, and we do try to keep the mythology alive. We are, after all, living breathing deterrents." His eyes get a faraway look. "I guess the program is different now to how it was when I was young. I was the first, so the early onset program was more of an investigation into me than an attempt to assist me.

"They just took the adult program with the legal aspects and the carrot and stick and added in a component to help me manage my urges until they were of use. They never tried to find a more appropriate outlet for me."

I nod, understanding what he is saying. India is being guided towards biology, she has an aptitude and it ties into his mindset. I wonder what St John would have achieved if he'd been directed like India into something enhancing, not prescriptive.

"Would you have chosen a different profession for yourself?" I ask, gesturing at all the ancient artefacts and texts around the room.

"What makes you think I didn't choose this?"

"I assume you were guided towards it, I just wondered would you rather do something else."

He shakes his head, "No, I am fascinated by language, particularly in the way it defines society and I am drawn to ancient societies, their most basic urges are closer to the surface, I like to study them."

"Does it not make your life harder though, working with things you are drawn to but can never travel to see?"

"My life can't be any easier, no matter the choices."

"But maybe maths or physics would have been less – I want to say emotional but that's not right is it? Let's say triggering."

"I am an obsessive, sweetheart," he says, "No matter the field I am always going to go all in and going all in means I will bump up against the restrictions around me. It would be stupid to pretend the walls aren't there."

Of course it would.

He leans back in his chair and I want to climb on his lap and give him some human contact because there is something almost soft in his eyes.

"Not being able to travel is the hardest restriction." He stretches his arms above his head and then folds them behind his neck. "I was reading yesterday about Leptis Magna, about the art there, the sculptures and the inscriptions. It's an ancient site that has been barely explored." He's right here in the room with me but his gaze is far away, in a land he'll never see. "It's in what is now Libya. During the days of the Roman Empire it was made rich by olive oil. Now it is hidden behind the dunes that stretch along the edge of the Mediterranean Sea. Leptis Magma, from what little we know of it, marked a change, a kind of blending of the aesthetic of the old Roman Empire with the influences of Africa."

I imagine low dusty ruins tucked down behind dunes, only visited by the bravest of scholars. Sin's voice paints a picture for me and he makes me want to go there too.

"At Leptis Magna the sun of Africa burns into the lines of sculpture turned more linear, less realistic, more plebeian, less classical, more expressive, than Rome, up to that point, tended to produce. It's where the world changed, just a little, and those are the places and times that fascinate me."

His voice is calm but I sense something hiding in plain sight in its even tone. The things he will never get to see, to touch, to experience. For a moment I understand his rage. His is a life imprisoned, and he never did a thing to earn his sentence. He was condemned to live this life based on probability, not fact. Something that would never meet the standards of guilt we insist upon.

"I would like to see the gladiator mosaics there," he says, "it would be interesting to see those in whose tradition I live."

I have nothing to say to that. We whisper in the program that our purpose is to help society evolve beyond the need to kill for revenge, but honestly, when Sin draws comparisons with Ancient Rome I wonder if we are watching the last flailing of a degenerate civilisation.

Sin drops his head, giving me the benefit of his amber eyes. It's like he can hear me thinking. He smirks. "Shame I can't be trusted," he says, "Which is interesting considering how clemency was such a roman trait. We see the blood they spilled, not the way they often chose not to."

I want to trust him. I want to set him free, give him clemency. Which is weird, because I don't feel like that towards my own sister.

With her I am relieved that she is contained. With Sin I am saddened. Which is ridiculous.

You know the tough thing about watching those nature documentaries - beautifully shot, gorgeous animals, empathy evoked? It's when the animal is in jeopardy from the predator and you are with them every step of their panicked flight, hoping and praying they will escape the greedy jaws behind them.

It puts a lot of people off watching nature films.

The guys who film those scenes aren't allowed to get involved. They aren't allowed to step in and save the young and the weak and the vulnerable. They have to watch through a lens while something adorable dies a bloody death.

That's me, as a steward, and it's also St John as an instrument.

We're the guy behind the lens.

We can't intervene, in fact we are forbidden from intervening unless it is very specific circumstances.

We need to see the kill.

Just like the wildlife cameraman does.

Only we're not watching a penguin in jeopardy, a stumbling foal, a cub about to be cannibalised by the new alpha male. We get to do this with humans.

I've got colleagues who think the animal thing would be worse!

I am more scared of that moment than I am about overseeing an execution, I always was.

I have no idea what makes me bring it up with the worst person possible. I should have brought my concerns about that to Rose, or Baldwin, but I didn't. I brought them to Sin.

"How do you do it?" I ask as we sit in his office and the atmosphere between us is calm and settled. "How do you learn to watch the killing proof?"

"You know how I do it. You are trained to know it, or were you out that day? Maybe taking your sister for a picnic."

"No, I was there, for that whole module." We spent six months on that. "I just was wondering how you did it, specifically, as you have been in job so long, long before the system was refined."

"So many sly little passive aggressive digs in there, shame they don't work on me."

"I didn't mean to imply anything," I say, frustration colouring my tone.

"Innocence is such an unattractive look on you." He drove me nuts, but then, he probably drove everyone nuts, it was his modus operandi. "I neither like, nor dislike, the burden of proof." He relents, giving me the insight I'm looking for. "I accept it for what it is, necessary, and part of the legal system I exist within."

I'm going to struggle with it, I know.

"I am held to a higher standard than all other laws, I am beyond reasonable doubt," he adds, "I am held to the standard of absolute proof. That is the requirement and in many cases there is only one way to obtain it. So be it."

"I get it, I do, but what if it's someone worth saving, someone who could have made the world a better place, saved lives?"

"You normals are so fucking judgemental, putting your people in little boxes, who is worth caring for, who isn't. I care no more for one of you than another."

I feel the sting of his contempt.

"There is no bias with me, that's the point. To be brutally honest you are all the same to me, just little bags of skin gassy with potential."

This was a really bad idea.

He gets to his feet and I can feel the room filling up with his frustration. "There is no defence against me. I see through all extenuating circumstances. I don't accept innocent by reason of insanity, innocent by reason of provocation, innocent by reason of some form that got filled in wrong."

"But you like it," I say softly, "That's awful, that's almost..."

I manage to stop myself from saying the word anathema but I know he hears it in my thoughts.

Of course he likes it, he is designed to like it.

"You even begrudge me liking my job, what a judgemental little creature you are."

He walks out of the room and I feel about five inches high. He's good at making me feel like a fool.

St John

Working with Natalie falls into a pattern, and I still don't feel the need to kill her although she got damn close the other day when she nearly named me an anathema.

She must have seen it in my eyes. I saw the fear and the regret in hers. It's why she is still here.

Fortunately I can walk past moments like that, but I don't forget them, I log them.

Natalie is now at my house most mornings and evenings, and I translate in the afternoons.

She makes the gathering of information about this killer interesting even though we are no further forward than an Enochian link after two weeks.

I am not used to companionship. I am used to working with Rose, but Natalie is different. She is funnier, obviously sexier, her energy tickles me and her body tempts me, and her smile, when it comes, is like the light in my house - clean.

When I kill, I'm alive. When I kill, I'm doing what I was made to do. When I translate, I'm working at what I'm good at, what Rose felt was the least damaging form of normal work I could do - because the discipline it requires keeps my brain calm. But when I sit with Natalie eating Chinese food, and she talks non-stop about books or TV shows or the case, it's a whole new perspective. I wonder how she is changing me, just by existing.

It is very different at first, but I find I'm getting used to it.

I haven't wanted to hurt her more than once or twice today, and that's rather unusual for me.

She actually made me laugh this morning. Not evil taunting laughter, but genuine, giggling, idiot laugh. What the fuck is happening to me?

Of course I get to lecture her regularly which I find amusing. She rolls her eyes when I start but she listens and she smiles in the right places.

"Language is fascinating," I tell her one morning over breakfast, "It evolves constantly. Lately the word *testiculating* appeared. Men normally use it, it involves waving your arms around a lot and talking bollocks."

That made her spit out her coffee and she had to text it to her colleagues.

We had a good day that day. I was relaxed and efficient because I had made her and the people she knows amused.

How very curious.

I am keeping to my routine though and my constant assessment of my state of being says I am on an even keel.

I don't sleep much, I never have. My nights are often slow though, and I fill them with art and learning, illuminating manuscripts, listening to Gregorian chants turned low because the irony makes me smile inside. The long white nights are when the monster relaxes and the rage becomes a background of white noise so familiar I can ignore it.

In the dawn I fan the embers of the rage while I train and fight and train again. In the common light of day and the bloody hours of late afternoon I investigate and examine the motives and the mean of the crimes they have set before me. But in the quiet of the hours after midnight I am the closest I get to relaxed - I just doesn't sleep.

These nights I find my thoughts turn more and more to Natalie. She makes me hungry, and I'm rarely hungry unless I kill. But she makes me want to eat between meals. To hurt her and fuck her, break her a little and see how she fits back together. That is not like me, but it's interesting.

My little steward, supposed to oversee me, although that balance of power has always been a little off.

Natalie looks up from studying the text she has on her laptop and her gaze meets mine.

I know my face is blank but I think my eyes must be talking today because I see her pupils dilate, her breathing get a little faster and I want to order her over, onto her knees, to take my cock in her mouth and hold it, nurse it whilst I work, keep it warm until I decide to fuck her.

She has called me anathema. She doesn't know the layers of meaning in that word, particularly to me.

With deliberate disinterest I lower my eyes to my screen.

Fuck off little steward, when I decide I'm ready for my next course of you it will be at the optimum moment.

Natalie

I meet with Rose for my regular supervision, to talk about my instrument and myself rather than the case we are working on and the legal side of things.

"Is he keeping to his schedule?" Rose asks.

"Yes, he seems to be."

"Meditating? Training, not that he dislikes training, it's meditating he is less keen on."

"I've seen him meditating," I say.

"Has he asked for a sexual partner since the kill?" She flicks her eyes up at me. "Other than you, that is."

I can feel her disdain, and it stings, it really does. I have never done badly at anything, I have always led the pack, and I feel like I am failing to meet her standards on this, that I failed from the get go.

"He hasn't asked for anyone," I say stiffly, "Nor has he had me."

"Don't get sniffy about it, you let him use you, you can't get blushy when it gets brought up."

"I'm not, I was hoping for more insight from you though, less judgement."

"I'm not judging you for sucking his dick, I'm sure he was persuasive, I'm judging you for thinking that he is off because of it."

"He's more difficult than I thought an instrument would be."

She looks at me incredulously. "Exactly how easy did you think any of them would be?"

"I just thought it would be more clear cut, you know, in how to tell if the instrument was unstable."

She shakes her head, looking disgusted. "I thought you were the best of a bad lot and now you tell me this."

I feel pissed off, I am good, I'm trying to understand, I'm trying to work on this.

"Listen to me," she says, as if talking to a child, "They are all 'difficult', they are all one bad day, one trigger, away from needing to be put down, but St John, he's been doing this a long time, his whole life, and he is the most stable of the lot of them. He has never been in the wild, he has never killed without legal sanction. His record, at this point, is better than your own."

"But he's hurt Stewards," I say, "He is threatening, he is obviously dangerous."

"Of course he's dangerous, he is meant to be dangerous." She glares at me. "In the interests of being utterly clear on this - do you consider your instrument to be out of control outside the remits of the program?"

"No," I say, reluctantly, "He is in control."

"Then go back to your fucking playpen, Barbie, and try not to piss him off, he is worth more than you are and he has proved himself."

She returns to her files and it is clear I am being dismissed.

I need to reflect on how this went because I am not covering myself in glory here.

We put more safeguards around these people than we put around the lowliest recruit with a fucking automatic weapon amongst the civilians in a foreign land. We break them and rebuild them in ways the average soldier would die from, and we keep them chained up, mentally. Sometimes it doesn't feel fair, but then I look into his eyes and I know, deep inside, is something alien to us all, and the chain makes sense.

Sin is out jogging, and I have the house to myself. I make myself one of his delicious cups of coffee and wander into the office suite. One wall is floor-to-ceiling shelves, full of books on symbology and ancient texts. It's quite the library.

Something tugs at my memory.

Library.

John Dee

Dee's library.

I shuffle around in my head. I remember reading an article, more of a list actually, a timeline of Dee, libraries were mentioned a lot.

We never did get around to visiting the library crime scene, it was a chaotic first killing, and Sin was more interested in the victim.

Something is tickling in my head. I sit down, breathe deeply, and close my eyes.

We didn't visit the library - I remember telling Sin I knew the place though, and I think I remember seeing Abi there.

What was it Sin said she was known for saying?

"Got no use for books, would burn them to keep me warm."

Apparently, she said that to everyone.

No use for a library.

St John is going to kill me, I should have seen this. Actually, so should he.

The connection between the killings and the scenes is Dee not Crowley.

The library was first, the observatory second, the sailor third.

I open up my laptop and pull up the bookmark I made on the timeline document for Dee and go through it.

The connection is there, it's tenuous at best, but it fits and opens up a whole new line of investigation.

John Dee had a lot of things to be angry about in his life, these killings represent just three of them. There are more. There are worse ones.

Dee was obsessed with libraries and calendars. He tried to establish a national library and failed. He tried to change the Gregorian calendar and failed in that too, denied because of the intervention of the church.

He was also obsessed with maps and navigation. He consulted on a project to exploit the newly discovered North American continent. That didn't end well; the whole thing turned into a giant fraud.

Like St John said right back at the start of the case, Dee was a polymath, highly educated for his time, and his interests were varied.

The Enochian symbols come, as St John pointed out, from Dee's original translation, delivered in Krakow and the phrase translates as *the true worshipper.*

Crowley wasn't a true worshipper; Crowley was never a connection.

Our killer, whoever he is, feels a connection with Dee, a personal and profound connection. So profound, that it makes him punish modern-day versions of those who wronged Dee over four hundred years ago.

A woman who has no appreciation for books, a fire and brimstone preacher, and a sailor lost on land.

My pulse thuds wildly with excitement.

I want to tell Sin.

I pause.

St John should have seen this.

Apprehension shivers through me. Why didn't he?

I don't want to lay all this in front of St John yet. He will not like this theory if I can't come up with more real-world parallels.

I flip flop mentally, gnawing on my lip.

A quick trip to the university, a scout around with this theory in mind could shake loose some ideas. The university has to be central to this; the kill locations reinforce that.

I know St John has told me not to do fieldwork without him, but this is innocent enough. If I can find a more substantial connection, it could cement the fragile team dynamic he and I are building.

Making up my mind, I leave St John a note and stick it on his computer screen. I pocket my government ID and grab my coat before heading up to the university.

St John

I alter the angle of my tie, pulling it a little looser and settling the knot a half-inch to the side. Make it look a little careless. Make it look like appearances don't matter.

I run my hands through my hair, tugging it into a tousled but appealingly nerdy casual style.

My face in the mirror is an eager but innocuous mask. The light tint in the glasses tones down my yellow eyes, making them appear innocently hazel.

Adjunct professor, my demeanour whispers. Researcher into minutiae. Last to leave the stacks. Drinks coffee from a thermos.

Harmless, totally harmless. Sweet actually, but so boring.

That's what the mirror reflects.

Inside, I am fucking furious.

I am going to punish that fucking steward until she pisses herself.

And she was doing so well.

A muscle in my cheek twitches, and I ruthlessly bring it under control. I board up the cage that holds my inner animal and promise him an orgy later. Right now, I have a role to play and a steward to bring to heal, not because she's wrong, but because she's damn right. It makes it worse.

So much for companionship and easy camaraderie.

It's turned me into an oblivious idiot.

I should have seen what Natalie saw. I should have seen it first, and then I could have made the intuitive leap that Natalie hasn't. I could have led her to where we need to be, rather than running after her and hoping she doesn't ruin it.

I nearly lost it when I returned home and found Natalie's note. Her thoughts lit a fire in my brain. It took seconds to run her ideas to their logical conclusion. It took only a few minutes more to find the next step.

I need to get ahead of her.

Once I've done that, I can devote some time to making her sorry she was ever born, or if she is a clearer thinker, that I was ever born.

She won't be the first.

I'm going to fucking ruin her.

She will learn to listen if it is the last thing she ever learns.

Chapter Ten

Natalie

I sign in at the university campus with my department ID and spend a few minutes on my phone wondering where to try first.

Thinking logically, I head towards the lecture halls that cover Mathematics and Physics; those were Dee's particular fields of interest. It makes sense that if anyone is interested in Dee's work, they will be associated with this department.

This part of the campus is unfamiliar to me; I only ever used the library here. I ask at the department reception for a list of today's lectures, and she gives me a printout.

There are two lectures currently going on, one is History of Mathematics, the other is Applications of Probability Theory (oh hell no!). History it is, if nothing else, it could give me more background information on the case.

The lecture hall is well lit and comfortable; this is clearly a popular class. I'm pretty sure I stand out in my suit and coat amid the more casually dressed students. I take a seat at the back next to a blond boy and pull out my phone to get some background info on this course.

The professor is speaking. "We intend in these lectures to give a brief introduction to the study of the history of mathematics. The potential subject matter is so vast that we can do no more than sample a few of the more famous and interesting topics, so I will be focussing on what I find the most interesting because, after all, I'm in charge."

There is a ripple of laughter. I look up and watch the professor.

"Of course, as the study of mathematics from a historical viewpoint involves knowledge of several languages, especially Latin, and sometimes Greek, as well as the ability to decipher ancient manuscripts, I'm going to make it easy for you and we'll stick to the accepted translations. We won't be going off-piste on language interpretation here; this is the introductory level after all."

St John would be right at home here with all his languages.

"Included in your handouts are a list of essay subjects you can choose. I'm hoping to inspire you, so we have subjects ranging from, Women in Mathematics, to Magic and Numbers in the Elizabethan Age, to The Life and Work of George Boole.

"Don't let me down people, I hate cribbed essays. You have choices here, let them fire your desire to learn."

The professor has got that kind of low-key charisma that you find on presenters that make hard science palatable for TV. Not intimidating, not weird, definitely attractive, but not overly gorgeous. The kind of guy who turns up in women's magazine polls on guilty crushes. There is a silver fox vibe there, and a lot of the front row is pretty, perky, female, and mesmerized.

He's not giving off a creepy predator vibe but I sense something there, something unsavoury but not obvious.

"You may be a little out of his usual wheelhouse," a voice whispers in my ear. I turn to lazily consider the man next to me, and I grin. He's wholesome and fit, with long legs in tight black jeans. He's saved from being bland by the cheeky light in his blue eyes. He rolls those eyes at me playfully. "His fan club is strictly sweet and obvious but his tastes are more complicated so I hear."

I raise my eyebrows.

"Just saw you looking, thought you might be interested."

"I wasn't," I reply quietly. "He's not my type. I tend to go for the cleaner cut preppy ones."

"And here I am," he says, and lets his gaze roll over me, "Ready to sling a sweater around my shoulders and take you rowing."

I snort a laugh and smother it when the professor pointedly stops mid-sentence and glares at me. I shrug an apology, and he returns to his point, his face clouded with annoyance.

"Coffee after?" I whisper.

"Love to," he replies with a smirk, "I'm Leo."

"Natalie," I reply, and settle back and watch the professor work the lecture with the ease of long-standing. He makes a dry subject engaging, I'll give him that.

Leo, it turns out, is funny as fuck. He's got a sly dry sense of humour and as a graduate student is a font of campus gossip. I feel like I've struck gold when he starts giving me the dirt on the Professor, whose name I have learned is August Scott. I'd laugh, but my Mama called my sister India so that would be pretty hypocritical.

The name rings a bell though, and I'm not surprised when Leo tells me the professor was famous for five minutes for a TV program he fronted which highlighted mathematicians throughout history. Naturally, Dee was one of them - *how interesting*, I note smugly.

Leo and I have coffee in the campus coffee shop. It's sunny, so we sit outside and soak up the relaxed atmosphere of this shrine to civilized learning.

Professor Scott, crossing the square, nods at Leo, and his eyes scan me quickly. I smile cheerily and give him a finger flick of a wave, kind of supercilious, because today I'm that sort of a bitch. St John is going to go ape shit over this when I tell him.

Leo sucks the cappuccino foam off his spoon suggestively and eyes me lasciviously. "I told you, don't bother, he's got a wife and you need to be part of a couple to play his games."

"Complicated indeed," I lean forward and give Leo the benefit of my cleavage peeping through the buttons of my shirt, "Exactly how complicated are we talking?"

"Undo another button and I'll tell you."

I laugh, it feels good to flirt. I'd forgotten what it was like after being in the centre of Sin's dark suggestions for so long.

"I don't think he likes me anyway," I say, nodding at the Professor's back as he strides away. "He looked less than amused with me crashing his lecture."

"Don't know why," replies Leo. "He's normally a more the merrier kind of guy, loves his lectures being packed, a real attention whore. He'd kill to get another shot at TV fame.

"His wife is lovely though, so sweet, I don't know why she married him." He takes a slow sip of his coffee. "And she's his third wife. Who knew Maths professors had quite so much luck. He is punching too; she's got to be twenty years younger than him."

To be honest, at this point, Professor Scott is zooming right to the top of the prime suspect leader board.

Then Leo adds, "They had a kid a year ago, rumour is that it's not his. I reckon the marriage is on the rocks. She's been looking distinctly watery-eyed of late, poor thing."

Congratulations, August Scott, you are now the key contender in this weird game of *who do you think you are.*

I thank Leo for sharing a coffee and dishing the dirt, but I decline to take his number when he sweetly offers it, and when he seems genuinely disappointed I feel almost grateful. Before Sin, I so would have taken it, and I would have called. Now I find I can't, and I don't know why. Before, Leo was my type, but obviously not now.

Undecided about what to do next, I decide to find out where the Professor lives. It might be an idea to talk to Mrs. Professor, see if she has noticed any changes in his behaviour.

A quick chat with the helpful reception desk, another flash of my ID, and I have the home address of one Professor Scott. It's on campus, funnily enough. It seems his post comes with a sweet little cottage on the edge of the campus, not too far from the access to the park. It actually backs onto the observatory gardens.

I'm going fucking great guns today. If I could have skipped down the path to the Professor's house, I would have. I know he is in the university proper, so his wife should be home alone.

It is only when I reach the red-painted door of the cottage that I suddenly think that maybe I should be going over all of this with St John first.

I hesitate, my hand raised to knock, and the door opens.

"There you are, Camille," St John says, and I stumble backward.

St John steps out of the door and then turns to the young woman behind him. "This is my assistant. She drives me – normally up the wall - because I'm utterly useless with directions."

He holds his hand out, and the young woman shakes it warmly. Her smile is sweet but her eyes are dark with tiredness. "Thank you so much for your time," St John says. "I'm so sorry that I called unannounced, but I'm only in the area for the afternoon, and I so wanted to speak to Professor Scott about the Tielhard journals."

"I'm sorry too," she replies, "five minutes earlier and we could have caught him before he went into his department meeting. I'm sure if you set up a meeting for next time you are in the area he will be happy to help you access the journals."

"Well, at least I got to meet you, and your delightful child."

I have never seen St John like this, so empathic and genuine. He positively radiates safety and comfort.

"Without your lullaby, I doubt I'd have got him off to sleep this afternoon, so I should be thanking you."

St John ducks his head modestly. "It was nothing. I've always been good with children. Now go, put your feet up for an hour, I'm sure you deserve a break."

She smiles and gives a little wave as she closes the door. St John turns to me and I know I am fucked to a fare thee well.

I swallow nervously.

"Time to go, Natalie," St John says, and his voice is different, cold, tight, yet vibrating with passion.

Or maybe it's anger.

Yeah, I'm pretty sure it's anger or more accurately, pure rage.

St John

Is this jealousy? I don't know, but it seems possible.

When I saw her with the preppy looking student in the coffee shop, laughing and laid back, relaxed and teasing, something inside me squirmed and whined, flicked its claws in and out, wanting to slowly draw themselves through flesh.

I want to punish the boy who flirts with my steward, but he is out of my sphere of influence. Natalie will have to take it instead, which is fine because she deserves it.

I never claimed to be nice.

I plan on leaving my marks on her because I don't get to keep trophies but Natalie, she is already mine. I'm not sure when that happened, but she is. She's mine, mine to punish and mine to fuck, and this punishment is long overdue.

Natalie

"Do I get a safe word?"

"No," he scoffs. "Do you think this is some sex game you would play in a suburban bedroom or a club downtown? This is fucking punishment, Natalie, we don't do safe words."

Sin's rage had been a white-hot but silent thing as we made our way back to the row house. He clearly took the time to stoke it.

Once inside, he strips off his coat and jacket, rolls up his sleeves, and pushes me ahead of him into the office annex. We bypassed the office proper, ending up in Rose's old bedroom, a room with dark painted walls and a thick carpet.

Now I'm standing here facing him, and I think I should probably be kneeling. I would be if I thought it would do any good.

"Will it hurt?"

"Of course it will fucking hurt, that's the point of punishment."

"I'm your steward, St John, it doesn't work like this."

He grabs me and slams me face first up against the wall. "Says who?" he grates in my ear. I can feel his cock against my ass, hard like a rod, pushing between my cheeks.

"Will it be sexual?"

"You think my cock is hard because it's decoration?"

"Just fucking tell me, Sin, what are you going to do?" Even to my ears, I sound whiny and fearful.

"You didn't tell me what you were going to do, Natalie. You didn't tell me you were going to the university, that you had an idea that turned out to be very promising indeed. You went stomping in there without any thought whatsoever."

I bow my head. "I left you a note," I whisper, "and you worked it out. You got there before me in the end."

"That's not the point, is it?"

"No." I feel like my throat is closing up. I feel guilty, excited, and terrified all at once, "But please, Sin, just tell me, are you going to fuck me?"

His breath is hot on the back of my neck. "Do you want me to, little steward?"

I nod again. I'll take the punishment if he fucks me when it's over because I want him; I really fucking want him.

"Oh," he breathes, and licks a stripe up my neck. I shiver. "That's the way the wind blows."

His grip on me doesn't relax. His large hands are pressing bruises into my body for the second time in as many weeks.

"Just as well that this is how it works," he says. "When I'm done punishing you, it's all over, there is no guilt. I don't hold grudges, so fucking you is very much on the cards."

A tremor runs through me and that must excite him because he presses closer.

"I'll take my punishment," I say.

"I'm so glad," he purrs. "Now strip."

St John leaves the room for a few moments, and I hurriedly strip. This feels unreal. I peel off my shirt and wriggle out of my pants. I don't know what to do about my underwear. I don't know what I am doing, period.

I can't believe St John is really going to do this.

I see-saw wildly between pants-wetting fear and complex arousal.

My heart is pounding, and I want to run, but Sin's right, I've fucked up massively. I did the one thing he told me not to do, and despite a brief note and a time delay, he still worked things out quicker than me.

I guess there is no alternative to experience.

And a killer's mind.

I squeeze my eyes shut and try to make sense of my scrambled emotions.

There is guilt and humiliation, but guilt is the dominant emotion. The humiliation is because I'm almost naked and I got caught being less than him, slower than him, stupider than him.

The guilt is the overriding sensation, but punishment will take it away.

Something that takes guilt away is worth it.

Sin steps into the room, and I jerk my head up and look at him.

He doesn't seem so angry, like my acceptance of punishment capped the geyser of rage in him.

He holds cable ties in his hands.

I close my eyes and breathe deeply.

Trying to be calm.

"Take your underwear off, Natalie. You weren't concerned about showing your new friend your tits, you shouldn't be shy about showing them to me."

I keep my head down as I reach behind me and unclasp my bra. I let it drop to the floor.

"Fucking pick it up and put it somewhere tidy."

My face is rosy read as I do what he says, and then I push down my black lace panties and step out of them, folding them in my hands and placing them beside my bra on the bedside cabinet.

"No, I'll take those, I may need to gag you with them."

I glance at him and he stands there with his hand out, imperious, cold and implacable.

I hand them over.

"Turn around, Natalie."

Obediently, I turn my back to him. He pulls my wrists together behind my back and slips the loop of the cable ties over my hands before pulling them tight. I jerk as they cut into the skin of my wrists.

I flex my shoulders and wait.

Sin's hand settles on my hip. "You're going to bend over the bed, Natalie. I'm going to hit you with my belt, and after every stroke you're going to apologise."

"How many?"

"Until we're done."

"I'm sorry now," I say, my voice strained. "I know I was an idiot. I thought it was something important, but I didn't want to waste your time until I knew."

"I understand the why, Natalie, I just don't happen to agree with it."

"Is there anything I can do to avoid this?"

"Is it essential that you avoid this? Can you not stomach it?"

I think.

"No, I can stomach it." I sigh. "It's just a little pain."

I think he smiles at that, because I can hear it in his voice when he says, "That's right, a little pain, and you'll take it for the team, won't you? For what we are building here."

I don't think it's a nice smile, I'm glad I can't see it.

His hand is between my shoulder blades. He gently pushes me forward until my knees connect with the edge of the bed, and then he pushes harder. I fold over, bending over the mattress and lay my face against the cold material of the bedspread.

I wait and hear the slither as he pulls his belt from his pants. Seconds later, it lands like a streak of fire across the back of my thighs.

Fuck, it hurts. I curl my hands into fists. The cable ties cut into my wrists and I bite the bedspread and fight back a shout.

"What do you say?"

I spit the bedspread out. "I'm sorry for going to the university on my own," I grind the words out, anger and humiliation and guilt swirling in me.

The next blow lands. The belt makes a cracking noise, leaves another line of fire in its wake, and I squirm.

"Again."

"I'm sorry for going to the university on my own."

The third blow makes me yell, but Sin doesn't have to remind me to apologise; the words are falling out of my mouth before I even feel the increase in pain.

The pain becomes a rising tide, and I ride it with clenched teeth, broken cries, and gasped out apologies.

I lose count after ten.

I only know when it stops, when the back of my legs are a mass of prickly heat and stinging pain. My back is slick with sweat, and my wrists burn from the cable ties.

The next thing I feel is Sin's hand on my buttocks. I freeze under it.

"Don't move," he says, and I feel his other hand slips between my legs.

The pain in my ass and legs billows like a sail, and Sin's fingers softly stroke the plump lips of my pussy, tickling lightly, sending different messages to my brain.

I gasp. The pain is still there, but arousal floods in when I remember Sin said he would fuck me afterward.

"Nice?" he asks from behind me.

I rub my face frantically against the bedspread, overwhelmed by the good sensations. I feel his fingers ease through my folds and my embarrassment notches even higher. I'm soaking wet.

"Yes, yes, nice, so nice."

"Good."

He finds my clit and teases it, circling it, tapping it lightly, and finally pinches it between his fingers.

I moan with the pleasure that fights and wins over the pain in my thighs. I cant my hips up, offering more of myself to him.

He pulls his hand away and I hear him lapping at his drenched fingers.

"You taste delicious." His voice sends shivers through me. "Sweet, with just a little hint of pain." One of his hands rubs down the back of my thighs, where the skin burns, and at the same time the other is buried back between my legs. Two of his fingers slide into me, going deep. God help me, that makes me mewl with pleasure.

He fucks me with his fingers, harsh and demanding and my body just gives way before him. He crooks his fingers, pressing down on the front wall of my vagina and I am gasping, on the verge of orgasming, my legs shaking.

He laughs and pulls back, leaving me shivering in position.

There is a snick, and the pressure on my wrists releases. I groan from that too, and pull my arms forward, rotating my shoulders.

"Roll over," he says.

Clumsily I turn onto my back.

He is naked – when did that happen? He is standing over me, and he lazily strokes his hard cock. His expression is admiring as he looks at me.

"Pull your legs back for me."

Gingerly I hook my forearms under my burning thighs and pull them back towards my chest, opening myself up for him.

He tilts his head to one side. "You're gorgeous," he says, "I like you like this."

He kneels on the edge of the bed, and presses a thumb into my exposed hole. "How rough can you take it?"

I shake my head. I don't know, and I don't seem to be able to speak.

"Cat got your tongue?" he mocks, "That's unusual for you. And I was looking forward to gagging you."

He reaches forward and flicks my clit and I jerk at the pain pleasure.

"Better make sure you can take a pounding."

Sin isn't rushing this, he leans in and takes his time, fingering me slowly, watching my body swallow his fingers, taking time out to stroke his gleaming cock and rub it through the soaking folds of my pussy.

I find myself drifting on the pleasure, rolling with his finger thrusts, gasping when his thumbs glances over my clit.

His concentration is intense, his focus on me feels amazing, and I forget that half an hour ago, this man took a belt to me. Even now, my thighs burn and the pressure of my forearms on my flaming skin is all too obvious.

When he finally presses his cock to my entrance, I am so turned on that all I can do is beg him with my eyes.

I freeze, still and trembling, when the head of his cock pushing against me. "Relax, Natalie," he says, "Let me in."

I cry out as the head of his cock penetrates me. He doesn't stop pressing in, sliding in, until he is balls deep.

He was big in my mouth, he's bigger in my vagina and the pressure and the pleasure make me writhe—God, so full. I arch into it and squeeze my muscles around him, so hard and so long inside me.

His hand lands on my thigh. "Still, Natalie." He drops his head, fighting for control. "So fucking tight, you're so tight. Keep still, or this isn't going to last long enough for me and I'll have to do it again."

I pant, adjusting to the feel of him. "I always considered premature ejaculation a compliment," I manage to get the words out.

He huffs a laugh then pinches a nipple and growls, "Not helping."

I throw my head back against the bedspread and groan when he pulls back and gives me his first real thrust.

Oh fuck, the pleasure is a zinging flash up my spine. It wraps around my pelvis, and I can't control the movement of my hips.

He thrusts again, with more power behind it and pleasure surges. Fucking never felt like this before. This is an orchestra of sensations. His thumb is pressed to my clit, his amber eyes bore into mine. I squeeze down on him again, feeling the head of his cock rub against my g-spot, and I see stars in front of my eyes. The tightening of my channel makes him growl. He leans forward, his hands on my knees, pressing me further open as he throws his hips forward, rutting into me with all his power.

He is close, I can tell. His cock gets harder, the flush across his neck and chest deepens, and the muscles in his shoulders swell. His eyes lock with mine, wild tiger yellow. I can feel him coming inside me, his hips jerking, the heat and liquid being forced deep into me.

He pulls out and immediately slams two fingers into me, curling them, fucking me hard while his thumb strafes my clit. My orgasm takes me by surprise, slamming into me, causing me to howl.

He finger fucks me through it, and then through my stuttering breaths I'm crying, I'm fucking sobbing, tears overflow my eyes, and I reach for him, needing him.

Making shushing noises, he clambers up onto the bed and pulls me into his arms. I cling to him and cry like a fucking baby.

"It's okay, it's okay, it's done, I got you." Sin's arms are around me.

"Jesus, what the fuck is wrong with me?" I speak into his chest.

"Nothing," he laughs. "It's natural, it's normal, it's human. You got overwhelmed. That happens. Come on, let's get into bed and keep you warm."

Together we shuffle under the bedspread, and I find myself being spooned by a serial killer.

I can feel his come leaking out of my pussy, but his arms are around me and it's comforting.

"I am so fucking sorry," I say.

"For earlier, or for the crying?"

"Both."

"Don't worry about it." His voice is right by my ear. "One is forgiven, and the other doesn't need forgiving. It's a very human thing to have an emotional release after an intense experience."

"You wouldn't."

"No," he admits, and his arms are warm around me, "I wouldn't, but you can.

St John

I had intended to hurt her, but when I looked at her with the cable ties cutting into her wrists, her skin pebbled with goosebumps, the guilt in clear in her eyes, I knew I wouldn't do what I had planned.

I would make her sorry, but not sorry enough to bleed, just sorry enough to be forgiven.

She was reckless, she jumped the gun, but she was also right. That causes something to swell in my chest, it's warm, like I swallowed too hot food, and it heats my whole inside.

As I gave her pain and revelled in it, the space inside got hotter and hotter, and when she cried after I fucked her, I realized what it was; I was so proud of her.

Good little steward, who gives it all up for me.

Chapter Eleven

Natalie

Sin and I discuss the case endlessly as we hypothesise and gather our evidence over the coming weeks.

In between surveillance of the Professor's life, Sin digs deep into his background, habits, and quirks. Every single thing he uncovers makes it clearer and clearer that this is our man.

We just have no proof. Not a fucking shred.

All we have are some crazy coincidences, and the hypothesis that a respected professor of mathematics is killing people who wronged a sixteenth-century mathematician who sparks his professional interest.

I can imagine Rose's response to this - "Yes, that makes perfect sense, now come with me; I have a nice, padded room for you to spend the rest of your life in."

We don't get to quit on stuff like this though, and we don't get to throw in the towel.

The story makes sense, even if there is no real evidence to support it.

Sin, putting himself in the head of a killer, runs ideas past me. He sinks into the case and weaves his scenarios while I make notes and run real-world checks. It adds up.

We climb a hill built of circumstantial evidence. The view at the top isn't pretty, but it's clear.

This isn't a profile, this is a story because, in the end, it's all about the stories we tell ourselves.

This is Professor Scott.

Professor Scott is greedy for attention. He is greedy for the renewed attention of the camera that made colleges court him and pretty girls hang on his every word.

Professor Scott is sexually voracious, and his favourite hobby is a little discrete swinging. He talked all of his wives into it. None of them were that way inclined, and the less they liked it, the more he made them do it.

[Nice little humiliation kink you got going on there, Professor. We see it in your not discrete enough online profile and the photos; she really doesn't look like she is enjoying herself]

Then the current Mrs. Scott got knocked up.

Nothing kills a swinging habit quicker than pregnancy, particularly when you add in a game of who's the daddy?

With a pregnant wife clutching first her uterus and then her offspring like a shield, opportunities for Professor Scott to indulge become nonexistent.

Professor Scott is up to front a new documentary series. It's been stuck in development hell, but they tell him that he is totally right for it, that it has mainstream appeal, that it's going to relaunch his career.

The documentary sinks into the swamps surrounding the glittering castle of Hollywood and the professor is furious.

He wanted it all and could almost taste that west coast fame while he lives in his east coast enclave to the brilliant mind.

[He hasn't got a brilliant mind, he has a mediocre mind, fame would have given him the acclaim that his career didn't. Without his TV stint, he never would have made Professor, despite his many attempts at genuine research.]

One dark night in early September, Professor Scott goes to his last solace, the library. He is a bitter, stressed man, sexually frustrated by a reluctant wife, sleep-deprived by a wailing child, and denied the acclaim he thinks he deserves.

Exiting the library after a fruitless night searching for something to revive his ebbing academic credential, she hears a whisper in the dark.

"I would burn it all to be warm, all those books, going to waste, when they could warm me."

Something in that moment triggers him. We're not sure what. But in that moment, he takes out his frustration and anger on someone who doesn't understand the important things in life. He kills the woman who whispered in the dark, smashing her head against the ugly concrete walls.

Here it is. Here is the moment. Here is where reality snaps. Here is where Professor Scott, with warm wet blood on his hands, dissociates himself from the act and seeks an excuse, a reason, a justification for his actions.

[We can never prove this happened but the brain, grasping at straws, in that moment handed him the role of John Dee, garbed in his light of learning, trying to show the world that libraries matter.]

Then something else happens, the traumatic event is compounded, the fury rewarded. The documentary opportunity rises again on the swamp tides, and there is hope, more than hope, almost a certainty now.

[I spoke to the production company. They have funding tied in, multi-country support, streaming services, and co-production costs arranged. I spoke to his agent; she thinks he's going to be super hot after this. I can't see it myself, but there you go.]

Scott saw this as a signal, a sign, proof of the intervention of a higher power.

The second killing is another spur-of-the-moment thing, but already he is evolving. He watches the ragged old man pacing around the observatory, muttering his brimstone and bollocks version of the universe.

He watches this one slowly strangle himself, a quick loop around the neck, a kick to the ankle to break the bone, a stamp on the hand to stop him getting free. Bodyweight does the rest, maths in action, how you don't need height to hang.

The next day, he is summoned across the country for a meeting. They pay his flights, business class; he feels powerful and right.

The unthinkable is happening, he will make it, if he can keep the higher power happy. Amazing what people will believe once they see a connection.

The second killing makes him confident. He is Dee incarnate, it's obvious now, it has a neat symmetry to it. Mathematicians like simple, and this is him being rewarded for balancing Dee's equation through time.

The sailor is third, just to ensure his future success. Now he adds humiliation to his kills, see the evolution? So fast. The humiliation aspect is for him. The killing is for the memory of Dee, trying to make stupid sailors understand cartography and navigation.

He plans this killing, this killing he lingers and enjoys. He finds he likes to watch naked men suffer, that's something new to explore, he likes that he can still discover things, dig out truths inside himself.

[His porn history changes dramatically after this]

Here is Professor Scott now, secure within his fantasy, waiting for his reward after having offered souls up to a higher power. By this point, he is utterly convinced that what he is doing is utterly reasonable.

"Who is next?" I ask.

"Could be anybody," Sin sighs. He turns towards his computer screen. The pale light catches his high cheekbones and threads silver through his thick, tousled hair.

"Dee had a lot to be bitter about, a lot to be angry about," I say.

"Indeed, but I think, given how fast Scott is evolving, that he will go for a facsimile of his wife next, should it prove necessary."

"Not Edward Kelley?"

Edward Kelley was the scryer, the conduit between Dee and the angels. He made Dee believe. From his mouth came Enochian. Kelley went on to fame and riches, Dee didn't.

Kelley is the logical choice.

I say as much to Sin.

He shakes his head. "No, I think it will be the wife."

"He will get to Kelley eventually, it is the inevitable end game, but Scott's not there yet although his feeling of synchronicity with Dee grows more compelling. He thinks he finds more parallels every day. My feeling is that he will go for the wife because that fits the time line. The angel "told" Kelley that he and Dee needed to swop wives, they did it, although Jane Dee had to be persuaded. I can imagine what form that persuasion took. That's why I think the wife will be the next target and I imagine Scott has already decided how to do it."

"Will he use his actual wife?"

"No, that's too real, too close to home."

"It might not happen if this documentary deal goes through."

"It will happen, he's too into it. My guess is that it will happen either way. At least any news on that will give us a heads up that he will act. That way, we can be there to get the proof."

He looks at me sharply when he says proof. I pretend to be busy with my notes.

He blows out a sigh. "At least we're working locally on this case. All this hanging around is much harder when we are far from home."

I like the way he says home.

When I meet Rose to update her on the case, she isn't alone. Baldwin is with her. I try not to stare at his scars, and fail. It's worse now that I know Sin, that I have been so close to him. To see what he did to another of my ilk.

Baldwin shifts uncomfortably.

"I'm sorry, I didn't mean to stare."

"It's okay, I don't mind people noticing, and it reminds me how close we all are to fucking up every day."

"Do you mind if I ask how it happened? I've been with him a couple of weeks now, and I need to stay on my toes."

"I think I caught him on a bad day," Baldwin says, and there is no rancour in his tone.

"Can we talk about the case, Natalie? I don't have time to listen to you two swop St John myths."

"Hardly a myth, Rose." Baldwin touches the thick twisting scar on his face, I think it's unconscious. "Your boy can be genuinely moody."

"You just weren't a good fit, Baldwin," she says. "My boy does fine with this one."

"Wish I had her charm then." Baldwin says. I like him, but I can understand how he would have rubbed St John up the wrong way. The play by the rules attitude would drive St John insane - and it clearly did. St John likes high octane emotional energy, banter and playing off each other. Brainstorming on his terms. He doesn't like having the rule book quoted at him.

"We've got a prime," I tell Rose, "but all we've got is circumstantial so far. We're digging on him and watching him constantly, but so far, there's not enough to justify execution."

"That's what I thought," Rose says. "How confident are you that this is our guy?"

"We're both really confident."

"Is St John getting itchy?" Baldwin asks.

"No, he's really focussed," I say, and he is, he's fascinated actually, looking for the evidence amongst the minutiae of the professor's life.

"That's good." Baldwin says, "He needs to be kept occupied once a primary suspect has been identified."

Rose agrees. "Keep him occupied between his courtroom and the motivation, and maybe some forensic proof will turn up before this has to rely on killing proof. Our forensic team is at your disposal night or day if you need to rush something through."

It's what I am hoping for because killing proof is my nightmare.

Killing proof requires either St John or I, preferably both of us, to have sight of the suspect taking another life in a way that can be tied to the previous killings.

It is a sad fact that the majority of Societal Justice cases go to killing proof. Crimes that lend themselves to routine detective work don't tend to come our way.

"If you need to talk about what it takes to observe that I am here for you." Baldwin' expression is serious and supportive, and I take huge exception to it.

"Are you here to give me a shoulder to cry on?" I snap.

"No, I am here as a colleague who understands the difference between watching the guilty get excecuted, and the innocent providing proof by dying."

Rose lets the silence between Baldwin and I stretch out. Guilt gives me a solid slap across the face while she waits. "Take help where it is offered, Natalie. I appreciate that I'm not good with the more supportive aspects of the job, and it would never occur to St John to offer it. Baldwin here has seen a lot, done a lot. We all need someone to talk to now and then."

"Sorry, but right now, I'm good. I'll call you if I need to. I won't forget."

Baldwin has to be satisfied with that.

I suppose it's a plus that they realise this could be an issue for a new steward. It does make me wonder if anyone ever offers support to instruments, or do they just assume they don't need it?

St John

"I know the steward you assaulted." Natalie is unpacking supper, it's Chinese takeout that she picked up on her way back from visiting India.

It takes me a moment to work out what she is talking about. "Oh, the guy with the eggshell skull." I recall the big steward with a stick up his ass, but not his name.

"Baldwin," Natalie helpfully supplies.

"Okay."

"I've known him a while."

I pull plates from the cupboard. I hate eating out of cartons.

I have a feeling this conversation is going to head into uncomfortable territory. I'm good with criminals and humanity's darker motivations, I'm less good with the fishing operations most normal conversations include. "He was too hidebound for me," I say, because obviously I should say something, "So I made him go away."

"Okay." Natalie sounds confused.

"You were going to ask why I injured him. I thought it would be easier if we got to the point." I peer inside one of the cartons; the spring rolls look delicious.

"That's your reason for slicing a man's face, scaring him for life, and fracturing his skull?"

I glance up at Natalie. Her face is creased in a frown. I pick a fork out of the drawer and twirl it in my fingers. "Don't worry," I say, "I don't find you hidebound."

"I wasn't worried."

"No?"

"Okay, maybe I'm a bit worried, but only a bit, because I don't think I believe you."

I spear a spring roll and arrange it on my plate.

"Don't let my approach with you so far cloud your judgment. I really am a monster."

"Yeah, but you're not that sort of monster."

"Fuck off, Natalie," I say mildly. "Eat your food, don't try analysing me, keep your skull in one piece."

"Hey, I just don't want to make the same mistake. I kinda like my skull in one piece, not providing a garnish to the fried rice."

She sits and begins to consume her food neatly. She uses chopsticks, and she's deft, her hands pretty.

"I had a bad week," I find myself saying.

She stops eating and stares at me.

"The week before I attacked Baldwin, it was bad. Rose got injured, and it was my fault. They assigned me Baldwin as a new steward. He was smug, implied we'd be long-term. He brought food, said it was for bonding, part of the relationship-building process. I made it clear that relationship building was on my terms."

I can see the thoughts flicker across Natalie's beautiful face. I don't understand a lot of them. We're not in a situation where my instincts work particularly well, but I do recognize the moment when she stops trying to make sense of it and files it away for future consideration - I do that too.

"Are there any spring rolls left?"

The topic change would be abrupt even by my standards, but I take it. I push the box across the counter towards her. "Leave me one more."

"Greedy!"

"Hungry."

"Mind if I stay the night? You want to go out to Anathema in the morning, and I can't be bothered to go back to my place."

The way she says the name of the estate on the Potomac feels easy, comfortable. She fits in there now the way she fits in here. We can move around each other in these places without feeling like we're stumbling through an intricate dance we haven't quite learned.

"Yes, your room is clean; I changed the sheets."

I know she caught the reference to her room. It's the first time I have called it that, rather than Rose's room. We both ignore it.

My steward is learning that discretion is the better part of valour.

I'm learning she sees the chinks in my armour but doesn't point at them and pick at them.

We're parked in the deep dark at the rear of the observatory parking lot. I heard today that the documentary is floundering again, so if Scott is going to seek another sacrifice to some higher power, tonight will be the night.

Beside me, Natalie is tense. This is going to be the hardest part of Stewarding for her. I can understand it; it makes me tense too, but for different reasons.

"What's the story with your sister?" I ask.

Natalie's mouth snaps shut, and her face goes blank. "Thought you didn't care."

"I don't care, but I am interested." It's another piece of the puzzle that is Natalie, so yes, I'm interested, and given my time in the program, I'd like to see how it has evolved, if it has evolved. I suppose it has, it's not like I'm a shining example of success. Dr Goodlove would never leave it alone, she was far too invested in its development.

Natalie looks torn. I know she wants to talk about it, fuck Natalie wants to talk about everything. "You won't use this against me, will you?"

"No."

She looks unsure, squinting at me in a suspicious way.

"I have many things to use against you," I say. "I don't need to resort to cheap digs."

That seems to reassure her as she turns in the seat. By the gleam of the dashboard light I can see the hope in her eyes, a hope of friendship, a desire to share personal stuff. It would make me sad if I could feel sad.

"My Mama had her late, long after she had me. I never knew for sure why, but I guess she wanted something to love because I was growing up and away. I was all baseball and college coming and nerding out with my friends."

I don't understand why people want progeny, but the idea of having something to love strikes me as patently ridiculous - get a cat. I quite like cats, they behave much like I do.

Natalie continues. "India was a difficult birth, they both nearly died. She was distressed in the womb, and they couldn't get her out quick enough, too late for a caesarean or something. They did say that maybe there would be some damage, but they wouldn't be able to tell until she was older."

She sucks the inside of her cheek. She does that when she is feeling things she wants to hide. I can see the skin pull over her cheekbone and her jaw shifts.

"I was my Mama's 'birthing partner' because we were a right on, proper names for vulva, kind of family, but they kicked me out of the room when it was going wrong. The next thing I know, I'm stood in a corridor holding this tiny human, and Mama is maybe not going to make it."

"No father around?"

"Nah, never had one of those, just Mama and me. She had no real interest in long-term relationships with men. She was a human rights lawyer; her work and her kids were her only focus."

"Human rights lawyer!" I can't help the huff I make, and I shake my head at the ridiculousness of it all, how life works out.

"Yeah, don't even go there." Natalie sounds wistful.

"So your Mama died?"

"No, not then, she got through it, but I spent a lot of time with little India while she recovered. I took six months out of college, which was fine because I was way ahead, and I hung around until Mama was stronger."

"Is this a very long story?" I am ensuring I keep my eye on the reason we are here. Natalie is interesting, but I won't let her distract me totally, not again.

"You asked!"

I roll my eyes at her, almost smiling, and she answers it immediately. Her smile is so ready, always about to bloom. "Go on," I say, "I'm just needling you, reminding you I'm evil."

She rolls her eyes in mimicry of me. Idiot girl.

"So anyway," she shifts on the seat, and even in the dark car, I see the way her curves enticingly fill the seat next to me, "India seemed fine, despite her birth, and Mama was okay, so I went back to college. And two years later, Mama died."

I raise my eyebrows, shocking twist.

She shrugs again. "She had some sort of blackout behind the wheel. Her car crashed, she hit her head, dead instantly. India was in the car with her. She was unhurt."

She shifts restlessly, but I don't press for further information.

"I was old enough to take parental responsibility. I shifted colleges, took up full time care of India."

I can feel the tension in her, vibrating, because something is coming, she is fighting to control its effect but the payoff is coming.

She takes a deep breath. "Everything was okay, for four years, until I got up one Saturday morning and India was on the back porch with the neighbour's cat. She'd taken the poultry shears from the kitchen and cut its legs off one at a time to see which were the essential ones for movement."

The blackness that lives in the deep depths of humanity is pouring from Natalie. I can almost taste it. It's like the ichor of the soul in pain. I've always liked it when my clients let it out; now I don't, because she doesn't deserve to feel it.

She sighs like a tree in a gale, and I get the uncomfortable urge to touch her. But I don't.

"What did you do?"

"First, I killed the cat."

I nod at that—the correct course of action.

"And then?"

She leans her head back, the faint light from outside catches the paler highlights in her hair, her gaze is fixed on the darkness outside. Mine is fixed on the darkness in here, in this enclosed space.

"I guessed what she was," she says quietly, "I knew straight away, but I went through the process, got her therapists - we had money, Mama left us well provided for. They all said there were issues, but they didn't want to label her because she was so young."

I nod again. I've heard that a few times.

"But I knew. Eventually, I bit the bullet and contacted the program. They tested her, and yep, my own little psychopath sibling."

"I doubt they said that."

"No, of course not, they said severe childhood-onset conduct disorder and recommended admission to the program."

"And you agreed to that?"

"If I hadn't, they would have gone for a court order, they made that plain, her test results were high."

She sounds defeated now.

"And so you joined the training program to be near her."

"Yep," she pops the p. "Me and India, we're the BOGOF deal, buy one, get one free."

I consider this information for a moment and run it through my experience of Natalie to date.

"But you like what we are doing?"

She looks at me keenly. "I wouldn't say *like* exactly!"

"Okay, human girl, you gain satisfaction, find it meaningful, have been challenged, stretched, and motivated by the process. You see the work you do now as much more than just a requirement of being close to your sister."

"Yes, Doctor!"

"And that makes you feel bad?"

"Why do I get the feeling I am going to regret this conversation?"

She doesn't need to answer. I know the answer.

"So how is she doing in the program?"

She relaxes minutely, past the painful bit, for now. "She's doing good. Her therapists and tutors are really happy with her. She's super clever and really into biology, so they are steering her that way. If we're lucky, she may end up in biological research - strictly monitored of course - but she could have a pretty normal life."

We both know what the alternatives are.

They hang unsaid in the air between us.

"It's good that they have a lot of extra options now," I say. I don't know why I am trying to be optimistic for her. "They didn't have those when I was a kid."

She turns and looks at me, her eyes so sad. "I guess instrument was your only viable option back then."

Now it's my turn to nod. "That, or the suicide option."

I'm not bitter. I can't regret the chances I was never offered. All you can do is take the options you are given.

I turn my attention back to the dark outside. There's a flicker of movement. "Head's up," I say quietly. Natalie instantly is with me, thoughts of her sister sinking back down inside her to the place she holds them. I notice this about Natalie, when she is there, she is really there, she can compartmentalise.

I catch a sliver of light in the darkness as Professor Scott lets himself out of his cottage. The shine of a night light through a slightly open door. I pick him out as he moves through the garden and onto the observatory road, heading for the park again.

We let him get ahead of us, and then we slip from the car and follow.

Scott is dressed in black and moves confidently. It's not so late that anyone would think it strange to see him, but they might notice the small rucksack on his back. I certainly do. It looks like our professor has planned to go hunting.

I'm surprised when Scott doesn't take the first entrance to the park. He continues down the hill to the more well-lit areas of the campus. Natalie and I trail him.

He turns right at the bottom, and I know there is another entrance to the park after the bridge. Plenty of vagrants bed down for the night under the bridge. It's an enclosed space where they can light a fire, talk, and drink their way through the coldest hours of the night.

It's also a spot where the bargain basement prostitutes hang out, hopeful of swopping a drink or a hit of oblivion for a blow job.

When Scott slips off the well-trodden path and down the track to the bridge, I put my hand on Natalie's arm and hold her back. We cross the street and loiter outside a late open bodega, looking in the window.

Five minutes later, Scott returns to the main path. This time, he's not alone. He has a woman with him, she's clearly an addict, rail thin and unkempt. Her bare legs seem almost unable to hold her weight and she stumbles frequently.

I hear Natalie's breathing speed up as I assess Scott's companion with my peripheral vision.

I'm pretty sure I know what ruse Scott will have used to lure this woman away, it's the usual one, and it's pretty much foolproof.

"Fuck." Natalie swears, and her body is tense as a bowstring as we watch Scott heading towards the second park entrance. It's locked at this time of night, but it's a flimsy, easy to climb over, barrier.

"Move," I say to Natalie. We cross the road and follow at a safe distance.

The entrance to the park is well lit, a noticeboard and plaque by the side has a floodlight above it, and a street light illuminates the gate itself.

Scott climbs nimbly over the gate. His companion hesitates, looking both ways. From the way she moves, she is younger than Scott's previous victims, but that makes sense. If this is the Jane Dee facsimile, she needs to be younger.

"What do you reckon he's going to do?" Natalie's voice is low and strained.

"Punish her, for everything."

"How though, if this is his wife?"

"My guess is something sexual and painful. Dee had to persuade his wife into sharing Kelley's bed, I imagine that he wasn't diplomatic about it."

The hooker has her foot on the first rung of the gate when Natalie turns to me. "Can't do it," she says, and I make a grab for her arm.

But she is gone, running wildly into the opening credits of a drama she doesn't want to see, making as much noise as she can, being as visible as possible.

"Hey, what the fuck are you doing? You can't go in there," Natalie's voice is loud and attention grabbing in the evening quiet.

I see Scott step back into the shadows by the side of the path as his potential victim jerks and stumbles at Natalie's shout, sliding off the gate. She turns to Natalie with her hands up, ready to ward off an attack.

"That's out of bounds, protected land. There's all sorts of animals and rare plants in there; we got to keep it safe." Natalie is babbling, playing at being a concerned citizen, badly, I might add.

I stay where I am and watch Natalie in the light.

The woman mumbles something, and Natalie shakes her head violently. "No, it's not short cut to anywhere, you could fall and hurt yourself, get lost and nobody would find you. Hey, look," she fishes in her pocket for money. "Here's fifty bucks, get a taxi or an uber home or somewhere to crash. You don't want to be out tonight and you don't want to be going in there."

I hiss, pissed beyond belief.

The woman grabs Natalie's money and hurries away, now moving surprisingly quickly on her stick pin legs. Natalie turns and looks into the woods, into the shadows and the dark, the streetlight falling on her beautiful, serious face.

My little steward couldn't bear to watch someone else die to be sure we had the right man.

Unfortunately, I can. Unfortunately I will have to.

I stalk towards Natalie.

Natalie

I see it in his eyes, the moment he goes from human to inhuman, from man to instrument.

It's always the eyes that give it away because creatures like Sin, they look like us, so much like us, until the mask slips, and the eyes go almost matt. It's like the light goes out, and the monster inside takes over.

It's like being transported straight into the centre of the uncanny valley, that place where the human looking and the human stare at each other across the sand and the human knows they are done for, they are outmatched.

Fight or flight? Or beg?

My hand is on the wood of the gate and I'm vaulting over it, into the park, onto the trail that Scott just disappeared up.

My feet slip on the mud and I glance over my shoulder.

Sin's teeth are bared, his upper lip lifted in terrible smirk.

I throw myself down the track, away from Scott's route, away from Sin, away from a murder that didn't happen – yet.

I'm trying to prevent another one, because my instrument is angrier than I have ever seen him.

Running becomes an unstoppable action. Once the choice is made, once my feet move, once I take that first lunging step away from him, my brain shuts down and my body takes over.

There is just cold night air, damp and thick in my lungs, the press of my feet into soil and the darkness in front of me, my only chance to hide.

To my left are the lights of civilisation, on the other side of the boundary, to my right the brush and the trees, in front of me is the stream, I know it's there but I can't hear it over the pounding of my heart and the rushing sound in my ears. Just like I can't hear the traffic, can't hear Sin, don't even know if he's behind me.

I veer right before the stream, the path jinking uphill, narrower, less travelled, stonier beneath my feet. I dig in, now not even sure if I can ever stop running because the need to get as far away as possible as fast as I can is whipping me on.

It's like I have been on the verge of this for weeks. Meeting Sin, becoming a working steward, seeing death and thinking about death, looking at insanity laid out in front of me, it has all been leading up to this flight through the night.

I couldn't stop if I wanted to.

The path grows steeper still, damper, and my boot toe slips, sending me to my knees, my hands scrabbling in the mud, trying to get finger holds in it. I push myself up, scrabbling forward.

He's behind me, I know he is, and he's faster than me, stronger than me, a hundred times more deadly than me.

The only way is to hide, I can't outrun him.

There is more light in the sky than there is down here on the ground. Washington's light pollution hides the stars but doesn't illuminate the park. I reach the top of the hill I am running up and just over the crest I go down on my stomach and roll off the path, slithering into the undergrowth, hoping the shadows and the textures hide me, hoping my move was unseen, unheard.

I lie face down in wet leaves and pull my hood over my head. I press my face into my arm and lie still as a log, my eyes squeezed shut, the panic that fogs my brain muttering nonsense to me.

If I can't see him he can't see me.

I know that's stupid.

It seems today is my day to be irredeemably stupid.

The skin on the back of my hands prickles, adrenaline crawling through me, and I hear his feet on the trail.

Light, fast. Don't look.

They pause.

You can't see me, I think inside the prison of my head, You don't know where I am.

"Bleeding hearts should know everything has a price."

I can feel the anger radiating from him.

Don't run. Don't move. Don't think too loudly.

"And the price you are going to pay will be high."

I hate myself so much. Why the fuck did I run?

"I'm going to find you and fuck you in the dirt little steward because that's what happens when you rile someone like me."

My nipples tighten.

"I'll hold you down in the night and take your body in a way that is nothing but punishment. I've punished you before, I thought you were learning, but it seems you need another lesson."

Don't look, don't turn your head and check, don't give yourself away.

"You will always give yourself away little steward, you can't help it, you're normal, and I can see inside you." His voice is so close. "I can taste your fear and your psychological pain. I like it." I bite my forearm, breath through my nose, soft as I can, fighting the urge to run again. "And I think you like it too."

A hand grasps the back of my hood and hauls me out of my hiding place. I shriek, I actually fucking shriek, and panic is like an electric shock to my system. I twist myself out of his grip, flailing wildly, all my training forgotten. He does that to me, he does something to my head, to my evolution, he sends me back into pre-history, and he brings out the primal in me.

He drags me off the trail and slams me up against a tree. I feel the bark against my cheek, cold and rough, and his heat against my back, burning through my hoodie.

I stand still, panting, waiting for what he will do next, and the panic bleeds into something altogether darker, altogether dirtier as I realise he is hard in his pants, the thick ridge of his cock pressed up against my ass.

"Bad steward," he says and his voice is like a nightmare, a nightmare where I do crazy things for no good reason other than the world he drags me into is very different to the world I knew before. "Running displays guilt, guilt can't go unpunished, that's the point of us isn't it?"

I can't speak. I can only hope this doesn't kill me.

I feel a sharp prick against my throat and I realise he is pressing the cold blade of his stiletto against my flesh. I didn't even know he had it with him. Thinking about it I should have, I realise now he probably always has it with him. It's part of him.

"How far do you think is too far to push me?"

"I think I have pushed you too far," my voice trembles, my teeth chattering although I am soaked in sweat.

"You are correct, you have pushed me too far. I don't know how you can redeem yourself."

"Take what you want."

"I always do. That's the point of me."

The blade slips lower, down to my belly.

"Stand very still, little steward, I'm about to cut you out of your clothes.

St John

Natalie shivers in the cold. Her bare feet in the dirt, her hands covering her private parts by reflex. Her clothes are shredded around her. There are tiny trails of pretty blood streaking her torso and thighs where the sharp point of the stiletto scored her skin as I cut her garments from her.

I am so hard I'm almost sure I could have cut them from her with my cock.

The thought makes me smile.

It's not a nice smile and Natalie tenses her muscles, trying to stop the tremors that rattle through her.

I stare at her, taking it all in, tasting the fear and regret on the air, mingling with the damp rotting smell of leaves.

Humiliation is a powerful kink.

I step back and perch on a convenient rock. I twirl my blade in my hand watching the edges catch the little light there is. In the distance there is the rumble of traffic as Washington goes about its business but it's muffled by the forest all around us. Wilderness in the centre of the city, the primal amongst the civilised. That's me.

"Come here," I order.

"Why?"

"So I can fuck you."

"Are you going to kill me?"

"I might, if that is what I want."

"Then no, I won't. I'll run and you'll have to catch me but I'm not volunteering for death."

"Alright, I won't kill you."

"You promise?"

"My promises are worthless, apparently I don't have the same moral code as you lot."

"I don't think they are worthless."

"Stop trying to sweet talk me and get over here."

She comes slowly, stepping carefully through the leaf litter and the twigs.

"Turn around."

Hesitantly she turns her back to me. Her shoulders are hunched.

I free my cock from my pants.

She hears the zipper come down and she shivers.

The night air caresses me. Soon it will be somewhere warm.

"Sit back on my lap."

She perches on my knees and I growl, wrap my arm around her waist and yank her backwards over my groin. She cries out and I press my blade into the side of her breast, pricking her.

"Did you ever think this would be what you were signing up for when you made your mind up to do your duty by your family?"

"Never in my wildest nightmares."

I force a hand between her legs. As I expected her pussy is soaking wet. Such a deviant little steward.

I spread my legs and force hers apart. I reach down and position my cock at her entrance. She is shivering wildly. I lift her and force her down onto my cock and she takes me whole length in one go, sucking me inside, her internal muscles rippling around me.

I groan at the heat, the softness, the silken strength of her muscles.

"Oh sweetheart you were made to be fucked when you are terrified."

She moans and collapses back against my chest. I wrap my arms around her and hold her in place, pumping my hips and fucking her roughly. My blade is flush against her skin between her breasts, the tip just under her chin and she arches away from it, her head twisting to the side.

I bite at her neck and fuck her harder, crushing her against me, grinding myself into her.

"I'm sorry, I'm so sorry." Her words are garbled.

"Shut up and take it."

I slide my hand up to her throat, holding it tight. I spread my legs even wider, leaning back and she is utterly impaled on me, crying out in a mixture of pain and pleasure.

I plant my feet and surge up into her, pulling her down at the same time. Her pussy gets impossibly tight, her hips stutter in my grip and suddenly she is crying out in shame as she gushes juices all over my pants, cuming wildly.

I groan and let myself go, my cock jerking in the grip of her spasming muscles, as pleasure ricochets through my body.

"Oh, fuck yes," My fingers dig into her breasts, my mouth bites down on her shoulder. My orgasm goes on and on and she sobs as she takes it all.

Slowly my heart rate returns to normal and my grip on her changes from harsh to just enveloping.

She cries, trying to smother her sobs.

I lift her off me and her legs give way, sending her crumpling to the ground at my feet.

I slip off my jacket. "Put this on," I tell her, "You'll get cold."

She looks up at me with shocked eyes.

"Which part was the punishment?" she asks.

"The chase and the cutting the clothes off. The rest was for us both."

Natalie

"Do you want me to fuck off?" I ask Sin when we get back to the row house. I'm wearing nothing but boots and his jacket but my car is outside.

"No." He turns to me, steps into my space, and without warning kisses me.

He has never kissed me like this before, it is slow and sensual, and his mouth is soft as rose petals. I sigh into the kiss and open for him.

His tongue leisurely explores my mouth, and I sag into his arms like some swooning heroine.

"I'm sorry," I say, when he pulls back, "I absolutely was prepared for it, but in the end I just couldn't. I had to warn her."

"It was a reflex, Natalie. You can't help being the way you are. You can train yourself to be different, but that takes time. Right now, you are still all human. And actually I like you that way."

"But you punished me."

"You ran, we all have our reflexes. And that doesn't mean we don't have to have proof, we still do."

I nod, I know that. I didn't save someone, I just condemned someone else.

He takes me to bed. To the room that was Rose's, with the dark walls and the wide bed. He is gentle and sweet, and he allows me to forgive myself when he sucks me to a gasping, rolling orgasm with his talented mouth.

"Why are you doing this?" I have to ask.

"It's what is supposed to come after punishment," he says quietly, "It is how it is supposed to be, isn't it?"

Chapter Twelve

St John

I set up the cameras while Natalie is out visiting India. The security at her condo is appalling.

Natalie isn't invisible; she isn't like me. She left her identity all over that campus when she first identified the Professor. Not only that, she has sat behind the Director in filmed and widely viewed congressional hearings.

It wouldn't take a genius to trace her, and our Professor is no fool. Deluded, deranged, bitter, oh hell yes, but stupid, not so much. It will take very little for his delusions to recast Natalie into his re-enactment of Dee's life.

All it will take is a check of the campus logs, a word with his student, the pretty boy that Natalie flirted with, and he will know Natalie's name. He saw her in the lecture, and he saw her again in the light of the park entrance, in all her beauty, framed nicely.

Me, I'm not so easy to see. I never use my name. I never sign what I can avoid. I never walk in the sunlight with my head up. Even in that crucial moment when I wanted to race after Natalie, I froze and stepped back. The professor never saw me. He will work out I exist because he will shortly know what Natalie does, but he doesn't know who or where I am.

Natalie, though, oh Natalie is right out there in plain sight. If we ever get out of this, I'll have to make sure that changes. I was stupid not to think of it before. Sadly, however, I'm not sure we are both going to get out of this.

Because Natalie dying will be the best way to ensure I get to execute this killer.

I don't make the rules, I just abide by them, as penance for being me.

Natalie's condo is full of photos - India as a baby, India and Natalie, and a striking dark-haired woman with intelligent eyes. Natalie and India camping, fishing, and horseback riding.

You tried so hard, Natalie. You just wanted to give her every chance to be a normal little girl. Shame she was a lost cause, just like me.

If I were a superstitious man, I would think the photos of Natalie's Mama watch me as I set up her home to showcase a crime in glorious HD. I'm not though, and Natalie's Mama is long gone, just like mine. It takes the sight of her bed and the faint whiff of her perfume to make me pause in my task. I touch the pillow where her head lies each night and try to think of another way.

I don't have feelings, I've been told that often enough, so that sensation in my stomach is hunger, not sorrow, I'm sure of it.

No feelings, only options.

I don't want to lose my steward.

I don't think this one is replaceable.

Natalie

India was an ass today, and try as I might, I couldn't get her to lighten up. All questions lead back to Sin, to stewarding, to killing. It was exhausting and left me irritable and frustrated.

Sin is keeping watch on the professor tonight, so I can just take a shower and have an early night and try not to think about anybody dying to prove a point. There must be a better way of being sure when we don't have forensics or enough proof.

There is a better way - the judicial system. But that doesn't solve the problem of the inveterate killer.

Round and round the ethics go in my head.

A headache nags at me and I just dump my jacket in the hall and head for the kitchen where cold pizza is calling my name.

Sin would be disgusted with me.

The thought makes me smile.

He's such a neat freak, and he doesn't even know it. Two or three showers a day, a spotless house, the only time he gets dirty is when he kills or fucks, and then boy does he revel in the mess.

The freaky thing about Sin is that he is so civilised. His house is beautiful, his manners, when he chooses, are perfect, his interests are cerebral. He will break off from investigations in order to discuss an ancient text with an overseas colleague, and he'll patiently, and with fascination, tell me the etymology of any word I choose.

And yet it's all a veneer, only a micron thick, and underneath is an animal.

After seeing him kill, and the way he went about it, never mind the aftermath - I have given up trying not to think about that - he is naturally staggeringly violent. Maybe, as they say, he is the worst of the lot, which is what makes it a total headfuck to walk into his office and see him standing over an illuminated manuscript, until you see the ink on his hands that looks just like blood.

He fills my thoughts, even when I'm away from him, it's like he has flowed into every part of my life.

I open the fridge and eye the dried curled triangles of pizza. This really is the pits. Maybe I could text Sin, and if the professor is settled for the night, we could go grab something to eat. My phone is in my jacket pocket. I close the fridge and head back to the hallway.

Some sixth sense that living and working with Sin has activated perks up. I pause, scanning the living room; something isn't quite right.

There is the smallest sound. I tense and begin to turn and all I'm aware of is a blinding flash of light accompanied by pain flashing along every nerve in my body.

St John

He was faster than I thought, and he didn't do what I expected.

I had expected Scott to set up to kill Natalie in her apartment, and I believe I was ready to watch it if I had to. My mind was an inky pool of intent, and I had submerged myself in it.

I am almost 100 percent sure I was prepared to watch Natalie die.

But Scott didn't do that.

On the camera feed I see him drag her unconscious body out of the apartment and into the lift but I didn't set up cameras in the parking lot.

I am hurriedly replanning what to do and how to do it when Scott's car pulls out of Natalie's building. I have two choices, check the parking lot to see if she has been killed there, or follow him.

Instinct makes me start the car and follow him. He will want to take his time, he won't have used the parking lot. It would be no fun.

I should call this in, and I'm more tempted to do that than I have ever been before. But I doubt assistance will be in time for Natalie, even if I call it in now.

I work out where we are heading within ten minutes.

Rage settles over me like molten lava.

The fucker is taking Natalie to Anathema.

He knows who I am. He knows where I am from. He has no idea how I will make him suffer for this.

Anathema is my territory, my land, my home ground, and he has my steward. Some things are not acceptable, some things cannot go unpunished, this is one of them. I am allowed this one.

Natalie

Consciousness comes with a shock, with cold water in the face followed by a slap.

I jerk awake, and I know exactly where I am, I'm just not sure how I got here.

My hands are bound above my head and I'm hanging from a rope slung over the beams of the carriage house. I'm also naked.

Scott steps into my field of vision. His face isn't handsome anymore because gloating isn't a good look on anyone.

The fluorescent lights have drained the colour from his face, and his eyes sparkle with madness.

"Hey," I say brightly, "don't I know you?"

The kind of fear Sin creates makes me submissive, fear of other people brings out the asshole in me.

"You will do as the angel demands, Jane." Scott's voice is deep and sonorous as if speaking to an audience. "It is your duty to obey your husband or he must chastise you."

It looks as though Scott is going full Dee tonight.

Scott has a cane in one hand and a scalpel in the other. He twirls the skinny lethal little thing, letting it catch the light. He doesn't make it look as beautiful as Sin does.

"Do we have to do the whole knife thing?" I ask, "Can't we just put an add online like everybody else?"

"Shut up, whore!" He slaps me across the face. "I see the marks of other men on you, the bites and the bruises. You will take Kelley to bed like you have taken countless others, and you will do it with enthusiasm."

"I don't think that's going to happen. Kelley has been dead for about six hundred years and necrophilia is not my thing."

The tips of my toes are barely touching the brick floor but I scrabble wildly at them as Scott steps close to me. His face is intent.

"It pains me to chastise my wife so, but an errant wife must be brought to heel." He slashes at me with the cane. Thank god it's the cane, not the knife. But the pain is no easier to bear.

The next few minutes are some of the worst of my life. Scott isn't random with his blows, some part of him not lost in the psychotic haze knows what he is doing and he chooses the most painful places to cane me, the most sensitive areas, with the thinnest of skin.

Soon my body is slick with warm blood and cold sweat. I realise I need to keep calm, keep my heart rate down, or I'm going to go into shock.

"Stop, you need to stop." I whisper to Scott.

"Why?" Scott seems surprised.

"Because this is crazy, and you'll never get out alive. My instrument will kill you."

"I'm going to kill him too," Scott confides. "I'm hoping he's going to make an appearance. I've heard all about the Angel of Death."

I know Sin has this place wired in every way imaginable. He must know I am here, must know what is going on. I just need to hold out until he gets here. Maybe if Scott takes the time to rape me I can survive this.

"I'm not your wife," I say desperately. "None of this is real."

"The angel is, the angel is real, I know he is."

"There is no fucking angel."

Scott slashes at me wildly with the cane and I jerk in the bonds as hot blood runs down my thigh. I can smell the blood now, metallic, harsh. I look down, and there is a puddle below my feet. I feel my heart stutter, I'm light-headed and woozy.

Sin won't get here in time. And then I realise that even if he did he couldn't do anything. I am about to become the proof.

Somehow, I'm okay with that; I made my choices. I chose the side that demands proof that makes *beyond reasonable doubt* look like a crack in the sidewalk. I stepped into this system voluntarily. I can't object if my death provides the required degree of proof.

I'm a lot of things, but I'm not a hypocrite.

The pain is overwhelming. It should drive me insane, like Sin, instead I sink into it, I let my head fall back and I look up at the age blackened beams of the carriage house.

I do love this building; it would make an awesome home.

I wish I had learned more about Sin.

I feel there was more to learn.

And I really hope India makes it.

Chapter Thirteen

St John

When I realise I can't watch Natalie die, it is a relief. The dam inside breaks with a sigh not a scream, because when Natalie's head falls back and her eyes go saintly soft, I know she accepts her fate. That's when I realise I won't have another martyr made in front of me.

A madman once believed I was an angel, it's time to convince another.

From my position looking in through the carriage house window, I can see that the professor intends to make Natalie suffer for as long as possible. Natalie is his wife to him, he'll want to beat her until he believes she will comply with his demands.

In Scott's crazy world view I wonder who is Edmund Kelley? Who does he want to give her to? Will he rape her because he thinks he owns her, or has he promised her to someone else? Someone who knows more about me than should be possible.

It seems that Scott has found his Kelley facsimile but Kelley was just the mouthpiece of the angels, repeating their words. I'm sure he would prefer an actual angel.

My back itches, the scars I mainly ignore tightening and tingling, the old patches of chemical burns rippling.

Time to use my ancient history.

I make my way around to the carriage house entrance.

The door has been forced, which was no mean feat, and it swings open when I push it.

He hears me when I step through the door. He turns to me with a bright smile, his arms splattered with Natalie's blood caused by the vicious cane strikes.

"HOATH," I greet him in Enochian, the guttural syllables grInding low in my throat.

Stupid fucking language, wrecks the voice.

He recognises me, and inclines his head. "Angel."

I ignore him and move past him towards my courtroom at the back of the carriage house.

I press my palm to the panel that opens the room.

The door swings open, and the lights flicker to life.

I turn to Scott. "Cut her down," I say coldly.

"Why should I?"

"Because if you don't, I will shut myself in here and you'll never get me."

"I'm planning on burning the place down anyway."

"This room is fireproof and bombproof. The demons of hell couldn't get in here."

"What's in it for me, Angel?"

"Me," I say simply. "She's a pawn, she is only a piece in the game. I'm the real deal."

"I was told you would offer yourself in exchange for your steward."

Now that's interesting.

"Really, so someone told you about me, that's how you know about this place?"

"Yes." Scott lifts the scalpel, and for a moment, I think he is going to slice open Natalie's throat, in which case I will peel his skin from him with it, square inch by square inch and make him eat it.

Instead, he cuts the rope that holds Natalie. My steward slumps to the ground, lying in the pool of her blood.

I hear her breathy groan. She lives.

"I was sent a message about you," Scott says, and he wanders towards me. I could reach out and snap his neck right now but this is getting interesting. "I was sent a manuscript, beautifully illuminated, it had little cherubs on the borders."

My brain overloads, images upon images pile in, short-circuiting my reflexes. My back burns and burns and I see the faces of the martyred, their soulful eyes, their crying ecstatic mouths.

I push the images aside, but I'm too slow.

Scott gets me in the neck with the Taser and the world flares into blazing white like heaven's gate.

I wake up laughing, because the program really shouldn't have kept me away from ritual killers, it turns out they have all the fucking answers.

The laughter turns to groans as Scott drags the crackling Taser down my naked chest.

"It's not funny, Angel," he tells me seriously, "it's not funny at all."

Scott obviously has some sexual issues he really should have dealt with by his age because I'm as naked as Natalie was. I'm tied to a chair, my elbows lashed to the back, and my wrists bound together. My feet are tied to the legs, and my thighs are spread wide.

Scott has left the courtroom door open. Through it, I can see that Natalie is gone. I can see the trail of blood where she dragged herself away. I don't think Scott has noticed; he's far too interested in me now as he wanders the far out lands of utterly insane.

"Why is your back like that, Angel?" Scott asks.

I smile up at him. "Because someone tried to rip my hidden wings out of my flesh. I nearly died the first time."

"Interesting." Scott runs the Taser lightly across the back of my shoulders. I can't really feel it but the muscles jump. "Are they still in there, your wings?"

"Why don't you try and find out, see what happens?"

Scott jabs the Taser into my ribs, and my body lights up with pain. The Taser is a pricey one, it's got a whole range of settings. This one is all pain and no blessed unconsciousness.

I howl, and get hard.

Pain always was my thing. Give it, receive it, I'm not fussy, I like it all ways.

Again and again, Scott hits me with the electricity. I laugh, and I jerk, and I scream because I'm not the kind to hold back.

I guess it doesn't matter who dies. I guess I can be the proof as easily as Natalie. There are cameras running in here. There are always cameras around me, I know that, even if Natalie doesn't. They never take their eyes off us.

I always knew it would end like this. I'm actually surprised I made it this far. It was certainly against the odds.

Now it's here I plan to revel in every nerve-shredding, mind-cracking, agonizing minute of it.

And I'll smile through it all. For Natalie, because dying is less important than finding out I can actually care about another human being.

I care about her. I would not have watched her die.

That knowledge is worth anything I have to pay for it.

Of course Scott will not get away with this, the evidence will be found, and the case will be dealt with. Rose will see to that.

The pain is glorious. If only this man knew.

I guess I am an angel because I can fly into the fire and turn it into something like a hymn.

And this is a hymn to pain.

And it is so worth it.

The singing in the nerves, the screaming in the soul.

I am so hard in my agony. Scott doesn't understand that, he wouldn't, he's just delusional, but me, I was created in pain.

I don't want it to be over, but it will be soon. Even my body can only take so much before it goes into shock and my heart gives out.

And then I'll be done and I'll have gone out in an orgasmic haze of pain. It was always going to be this way.

I'm so glad I met Natalie before the end. I am so happy that Natalie survives. I'm so glad I didn't have to watch her die—my beautiful little steward.

Natalie

I am weak, so fucking weak. The edges of my vision are black and I'm fighting the clinging hands of unconsciousness. They have me tight, they are pulling me under, but I'm not going without a fight.

The blood is an incentive. I want to get away from it, get out of the gluey feel of it on my skin, the smell of it in my nostrils.

Slowly, painfully, I drag myself out of the line of sight of the courtroom. I can hear Scott inside, slamming cabinet doors and the scrape and screech as he pulls something across the floor.

I refuse to look at the blood. I won't be distracted by the blood. I can feel it seeping sluggishly from the cane strikes but if I last long enough, it will clot. My body will do its job; none of these are killing wounds.

Painfully, I force myself up onto my knees. I rest a moment, breathing quietly, and I hear Sin start laughing.

I edge towards the courtroom door, the bright-lit rectangle calling to me - come into the light. I smother a giggle at that. Most people stay away from the light.

I hear Sin growl something about wings, and then he starts screaming. It's like someone poured salt in my wounds because my body flails at the agony in his voice.

I manage to get my feet under me, and I stumble towards the courtroom door.

Sin screams and screams and suddenly it sounds like music, like a hymn. I'm really fucking delusional now.

I fall against the courtroom room, slumping. I scrabble for the emergency button, my fingers slick with blood.

Sin's scream is an anthem, a driving force.

I push, slide the panel down and press the button inside.

As I push it, I fall into the room and the door slams shut behind me.

I look across at St John, his eyes are luminous yellow, evil incarnate. Scott, standing over him, gapes at me, and starts across the room.

I see St John take in a deep breath. He bends forward and twists his upper body, first one way and then the other. I actually hear his shoulders dislocate.

A spray is pumping out of the high vents around the room. It's wet on my face, and everything starts to swim in front of my eyes.

I look at St John. It looks as though he has wings growing out of his back. His shoulder blades are high and wrong, but he is standing, pulling himself loose from his bonds, twisting and flexing, forcing his shoulders back into place.

The anaesthetic aerosol drifts down like angel tears. I breathe it in. It smells sweet but tastes bitter.

Both Sin and Scott fall to their knees.

I blink, blackness washes across my vision.

The last thing I see is Sin crawling towards Scott, his face a rictus of pain. His yellow eyes flare through the falling mist of the aerosol - *something wicked this way comes*, I think before the lights go out.

Chapter Fourteen

Natalie

"That was quite the scene at the end," Rose says.

It's a week later. I'm healing well, although not as fast as St John who shook off a double shoulder dislocation and enough pain to drive a man insane in twenty-four hours.

I move uncomfortably in my chair. "I could have done without Baldwin finding Sin and I naked and wrapped around each other like babes in the wood."

"He appears only mildly traumatised." Rose taps her desk with a pen. "Do you know what happened at the end? How St John snapped Scott's neck?"

"You don't know?"

"No," she shakes her head. "St John is refusing to talk about it, and the aerosol obscured the cameras."

"I didn't even know there were cameras in there."

"Most stewards don't know. We don't like them to know we have such oversight. The tapes are wiped every twenty-four hours. We only have them for investigative purposes. They aren't monitored."

"I have no idea how he killed Scott," I say. "I know he did it, but I didn't see it."

Rose shrugs. "Doesn't matter I suppose. We have always known that St John has huge reserves of strength, his pain threshold is ridiculously high, and his ability to perform under stress is unmatched."

"Still, that was pretty much beyond human."

"Maybe he really is an angel," she says.

"For fuck's sake don't let him hear you say that!"

She laughs. "And what about you, Natalie? What do you want to do now?"

"I'm going to keep on working with Sin if he still wants me."

St John had been somewhat less than welcoming when I saw him in the hospital. He had been withdrawn and wouldn't meet my eyes.

"He has asked to be assigned a new steward."

Something inside me cries out in pain.

"I refused his request," Rose adds. "He needs to work through his issues. I can imagine what his issue is with you, but he doesn't get to dictate everything."

"We certainly have some things to talk about," I say, "but I really want to keep working with him."

"He has a beautiful mind," Rose says, a faraway look in her eyes. "It has such depths, you could spend a decade just swimming in the shallows. If you chose to."

"Even though it might kill me."

"I doubt it, so long as you are careful."

"Most relationships don't work like that," I point out.

"Normal ones don't, but you are no more normal than he is," she says, hope in her tone. "Out in the real world, you and St John would never work, you would kill each other, no questions asked, but here, in this world, in this very false, very restricted, very bizarre world, someone like you can forge a deep relationship with someone like him."

"It sounds like you really love him," I say.

"No, I could kill him tomorrow," she replies bluntly. "I would be sorry I had to, but I could do it."

"But you raised him, worked with him for decades."

"Yes, but I am not you. I cannot love what St John is."

"But you think I can. That I do."

"You love your sister, don't you?"

"Yes, but she's my sister, I'm programmed to love her."

"Would you turn your back on her on any given day?"

"Well, no, that would be stupid."

"But you wouldn't kill her, would you?"

"No."

"Then you have your answer, Natalie," she says seriously.

I pause. "Looks like I'm back with Sin then, but I don't think he's going to make it easy on me. He doesn't like his desires being denied."

"I could send him a string of Stewards just to remind him how much more annoying they are than you, but that would decimate the graduating class," Rose says, "and as much as I like practical, painful lessons, the paperwork would be atrocious."

I arrange to meet St John in the park by headquarters, the one with the pretzel statue. I think neutral ground is best for us at this point. We can work up to being in each other's spaces again.

He reluctantly agrees.

I spend some time with India while I wait for St John. Her tutor is with her, and India winds her up about the pretzel statue while I lean against it and buy into India's quirky ideas. Is it actually possible to have a stick with one end?

It is important that I go back into the field with St John. It's important that we get over our issues - I'm pretty sure he was prepared to watch me die to get the killing proof, and now he doesn't want to face me. I'm not letting that stop me.

I need to learn more about the system, about Instruments and Stewards. Unless I know more, I can never hope to make the future better for India.

I see Sin approaching. His hands are in his pockets, his collar is turned up. The sharp winter wind catches his hair ruffling it. I raise a hand, he nods at me and hangs back.

India and St John aren't allowed to meet, but I call India over and point St John out to her.

St John and India seem to recognize something in each other. They nod gravely and with respect at each other.

I wait until India's tutor takes her inside before I approach Sin.

"How are you?"

He shrugs. "Fine."

"I know you were willing to let me die." I generally find it is best to get straight to the point with St John. "That doesn't bother me, it shouldn't bother you, it doesn't affect our working relationship."

St John shakes his head. "That's not the issue. I was prepared to let you die, then I decided that I couldn't. I have no problem with either of those decisions."

"What is the problem then?"

"I can't tell you that."

"Why not."

"Because it's a secret." Sin looks frustrated as hell by having to say that sentence.

I laugh at him. "Because it's a fucking secret?" I say incredulously. "What are you, six years old?"

Sin looks mutinously at me. "It is a dangerous secret," he mutters.

"Oh, well, that's something," I say, and smile at him.

My tiger, my deadly, dangerous, unearthly tiger. I saw him crawl through his own pain to kill a man. I heard him scream like angels singing.

I am fascinated and entranced by him. I find him funny, frightening, erudite and educated, and sexy as hell.

He has fucked me, hurt me, sacrificed me, and saved me.

I'm not done with him yet.

And I'm not letting him be done with me.

I could say, in the well crafted words of the great Aaron Sorkin, that my demons are shouting down the better angels in my brain but I didn't know I had any demons, until they stepped out of my mind and stood in front of me. I thought I was the angel. Now I realise there are no angels, there are just people, and the voices in their heads aren't angels or demons, they are just us, evolving away our days. We are selfish and needy, fearless and opinionated, angry and entitled, and we will be vengeful and fair until finally we achieve, if not enlightenment, then peace.

It's the best we'll get. And if I keep feeling the way I do for this man it will never happen for me.

For the first time ever I reach out and touch him first. Giving into temptation, I brush my thumb over his lower lip. He gazes at me with shadowed yellow eyes.

"Your dangerous secret is my dangerous secret," I tell him. Then, taking my life in my hands, I lean in and kiss him.

He sighs under my kiss, and his strange eyes flutter shut, so I take advantage and deepen the kiss until he takes over, pushing back and taking my mouth just the way I want him to.

We have a long way to go, my instrument and I, but I'm on this path with him, until the very end.

The End.

Natalie and St John with return in Book Two of the Just Deserts Series – Anomaly – where more of Sin's traumatic past will be uncovered.

Author Bio - About Gwen Day

Gwen Day is a storyteller who loves all the tropes - opposites attract, friends to lovers, enemies to even hotter lovers, age gap, second chance (total fave). She likes her heroes complex, her heroines bright, and has recently appeared to have developed a thing for men in kilts.

She is mainly fueled by tea. not posh tea, any old tea, buckets of it.

You can find her on TikTok[1] and Facebook[2] – come and say hello.

And you can subscribe to her newsletter for freebies, news and extras here - Newsletter[3] She promises not to spam you.

---

1. https://www.tiktok.com/@gwendayauthor?is_from_webapp=1&sender_device=pc

2. https://www.facebook.com/profile.php?id=100086451562029

3. https://bookhip.com/WZKRBJQ

Gwen's other novels

<u>Say Red - Exposed Desires Book One</u>[1]

Arrangements Inc - catering to all your secret fantasies - by negotiation, and at a price.

I thought selling myself was a painless way to deal with a painful situation.

He thought buying my time was the best way to scratch his particular kind of itch.

I thought the test that said I belonged on my knees in front of him was hogwash.

He thought he could see right through me, and the test told him all he needed to know.

I thought I was a decent girl doing dirty things for selfless reasons.

He thought paying a fortune for it made it clean and simple.

We were both wrong, on all counts.

We were layers of desires and fantasies slowly revealing themselves to each other - his praise made me weak at the knees, my drive to please him sent his possessiveness into overdrive.

Someone needed to Say Red before we both got burned, and neither of us would say a thing.

SAY RED[2] is the first book in the Exposed Desires Series, where everyone finds out exactly what gets them hot, and how much it will cost them to experience it. Expect plenty of bossy alpha men, steamy exploration, and HEAs in these high heat romance

---

1. https://books2read.com/u/mVA60p

2. **https://books2read.com/u/mVA60p**

<u>Say Please - Exposed Desires Book 2</u>[3]

Arrangements Inc - providing perfect partners, no matter how extreme your needs.
I insisted the boyfriend experience was what I did best.
She insisted a manufactured dominant couldn't match her wild heart.
Arrangements Inc didn't agree
I was sure I was a good man and good men don't dominate
She was sure it would take more than one man to meet her complex needs
Arrangements Inc didn't agree
I was determined that if I was doing this I was doing it by the book.
She was determined to break me open and show me I couldn't handle her.
Arrangements Inc said that was up to us.
We were a perfect match trying to prove everyone wrong. Me with my darkness tucked deep inside, her with her kaleidoscope needs right out there in the open.

---

3. https://books2read.com/u/bQjJNv

We should have been saying thank you instead of trying to make the other break.

Say Please[4], is the second book in the Exposed Desires series. It's the story of Mani and Ryker, a wild genius girl and a laid back good guy wrestling with his dark desires. Expect high heat, plenty of hot exploration, and a HEA in this adult romance.

---

4.   https://books2read.com/u/bQjJNv